A DIFFERENT HUSBAND

A Robeson Family Novel
Book 3

CHRISTINE MICHELLE

www.sophenebooks.com

SOPHENE

About the Book

NOTE FROM AUTHOR AND TRIGGER WARNINGS

COURTNEY

I always thought Beckett was the man who I would marry. He had been my everything since we were 10. We were engaged by the time I turned 22.

Then, one day, he came to me with a plan to help save his cousin's inheritance. It would make me the villain of the story in everyone else's eyes. It would also mean that walk down the aisle would happen with the wrong man.

Still, Beckett asked. I granted him this crazy scheme, played along, and quickly learned that he had agreed to it because it freed him from me for a little while. I never knew he wanted out. He never let on until I had a different husband's ring on my finger and was forced to watch from the sidelines as Beckett carried on with other women.

Flynn's was the shoulder I leaned on, and we grew closer as a result. Eventually, Beckett began to notice me again, but somewhere along the line, things changed. When I saw my future, he was no longer the man wearing the ring that matched my own.

FLYNN

My cousin won our mutual best friend's heart long ago.
I'd hated him for it then.
I hated him for allowing her to marry me 'temporarily' even more.
I'd always been a little in love with Courtney, but watching as the light left her eyes when her fiancé threw her away and paraded other women in front of her, made me want to show my beautiful new wife what it was like to be with the right Robeson man. I wanted to bring her light back. The only problem was, I had to do it before my cousin realized just how badly he had screwed up by letting her go in the first place.

*A Different Husband is the third book in the Robeson Family Novels, but it is a standalone story. The Robeson Family Novels can be read in any order. There is no cheating by main characters, despite the arranged marriage.

NOTE FROM THE AUTHOR:

When I first planned the three Robeson siblings' books, the original timeline was to release When the Last Petal Falls, A Different Husband, and then The Forgotten Wife.
Mina was a typical youngest sibling, and demanded her time to shine first, so the stories are told a little out of order.

If you want to read them according to the timeline:

When the Last Petal Falls
A Different Husband
The Forgotten Wife

If you want to read them in the order they released:

The Forgotten Wife
When the Last Petal Falls
A Different Husband

It doesn't matter which order you read them in, as they all stand alone and only give little mentions of the other siblings in their own books, but I wanted to be sure everyone knew, as you won't see Mina married to Tucker yet in the beginning of this book.

TRIGGER WARNINGS

Betrayal by love interest (not a main character)
Betrayal by family
Intimate scenes between adults
Strong language
Cheating (not by main characters)
Unexpected pregnancy
Drinking

For Maya, who gave me wine advice because I'm the heathen friend whose palette only extends to Moscato.
For Christy - my lifesaver, my bestie, the one person who knows my crazy process and doesn't judge me for it.
For Peggy who made the words work and puzzled through the weird document gremlins with me.

Chapter One

COURTNEY

"I NEED you to marry Flynn instead of me at our wedding."

My fiancé's words didn't register because I was too concerned with the fact that my mother wanted me to use silver and purple as our wedding colors. They had been our elementary and high school colors, and she thought it would be adorable that we marched into the future while paying homage to the roots of our love story. In theory, it sounded great, but my eyes continued to dart back to the pictures of the beautiful peach floral arrangements that were sent to me last week.

My wedding was only a few weeks away and everything needed to be finalized. The flowers and cake were the final items, and they were only still on the to-do list because I couldn't pick a complementary color. Silver was a given. Peach was my choice, purple my mother's. I continued to stare at the peach floral arrangement as I tried to wrap my head around what Beckett had just asked of me.

"I'm sorry, you need me to do what?" I asked the question as I blinked rapidly in an attempt to unsee the man standing before me, considering he had just asked me to do the unthinkable.

Beckett Robeson, the man I'd been a little bit in love with since all the way back in elementary school, did not change what he said, nor did what I thought was a waking nightmare end. Instead, he grinned down at me as he took my hands into his own and made me a stupid promise.

"Everything will be fine. Flynn just needs to know that it's someone the family can trust. I promise, all of this," he offered as he let go of my hand with one of his in order to sweep over the wedding plans I'd meticulously crafted – *our* wedding plans – "can wait until after we help Flynn."

"Beckett?" I questioned, but he continued to grin at me like a complete freaking idiot. His slightly wavy hair had come free of the gel he used to slick it back. As it flopped down into his eyes again, I realized just how nervous he must have been for the conversation. He only ever pushed his hands through his hair when his nerves got the best of him. Still, I couldn't fathom him ever getting himself worked up about this particular issue. My fiancé wanted me to marry his cousin instead. Even if it was a temporary arrangement, how could he even suggest that?

"You can't be serious."

My fiancé sat down beside me, and once again took both of my hands in his. I wanted him to appear forlorn over this situation, or at the very least, a bit put out by the demands of his family. Instead, there was an excited gleam in his eyes that looked a lot like giddiness. The man who was supposed to love me forever shouldn't seem triumphant about asking me to marry someone else.

"Courtney, you have to understand, it's not just about

what Flynn stands to gain. Hell, the crazy bastard was willing to give it all up. The problem is that his family's business is also on the chopping block if he doesn't settle the terms of our grandfather's Last Will and Testament. I told you that Grandfather didn't include me as the backup. I can't inherit any of it. I don't think Flynn knows that either, or at least he hasn't realized yet. This way, maybe I can get him to sell me the cabin. You know what it means to me."

"I understand all that, Beckett. What I don't understand is why I have to be *that* person. We were planning our own wedding." I pulled my hand free from his and lifted the pictures of table settings I'd been going through. "These were supposed to be for us, *our* memories. This was *MY* dream wedding." My voice took on a pleading tone as I stared into his caramel-colored eyes and practically begged him to change his mind and not ask this of me. When he said nothing, I continued. "*Our* wedding! *Our* memories! Doesn't that mean anything to you?"

"Sweetheart, I know you've worked hard on this, but that's also what makes it perfect. All the details are already set. All you have to do is show up and say your vows to my cousin instead of me."

He shrugged his shoulders as if it really weren't that big of a deal. Instead of him being my one and only by the time we got married, I would be divorced from someone else if I went along with this crazy plan to marry his cousin. It made my heart ache just to think of it. Beckett had truly been my one and only. He was my first everything and I was his. I couldn't imagine saying, 'I do' to anyone else, for any reason.

"But then my dream wedding and all this planning will

be for someone else. Then what am I supposed to do for our wedding?"

Once again, my eyes tracked the up and down motion of his shoulders. The indifferent gesture killed something deep down inside of me. If I had to put a finger on what that thing was that died, I'd say it was my hope. The twinkle in his eyes made Beckett seem younger than his 25 years somehow. We had been middle school sweethearts, though I'd loved him long before that. We continued our relationship all through high school. I waited to be married to him until he had his MBA, just as we planned. This was finally supposed to be our time to make everything as official as it could be. So, why did my fiancé seem happy to hand me off to his cousin instead?

"What does Flynn have to say about all this?"

Beckett chuckled. "Flynn didn't think I'd be able to convince you to do it."

The three of us had grown up together, gone to school together, and had known one another since Flynn was pulled out of his stuffy private academy in middle school. After moving to slum it with the rest of us in public school, Beckett's cousin had become a third wheel whenever we would hang out. I knew Flynn and liked him just fine. He had even been one of my best friends for the longest time, but he wasn't the boy I always dreamed of marrying. He knew me well enough to know that I wouldn't want any part of this, so why didn't my own fiancé know the same thing?

"What if I said 'no'?" The determined look in Beckett's eyes said everything I needed to know. He would be angry with me if I didn't go along with this scheme.

"Come on, Sweetheart. It's not forever."

"It is a legally binding marriage, Beckett!"

"Meh!" He made the noise in an exaggerated, exasperated way that grated on my nerves. "Courtney, do this for me, for us, for our future children."

"What are you going on about? Why would this be good for our future children?"

My fiancé rolled his eyes at me again, as if I should already know the answer. "Flynn plans on compensating you for your time and trouble."

I gasped. "This is about money?" I had gone to school to be an art teacher. What I really wanted to do was to one day become a successful artist in my own right, but until that day, I could teach other children out there who had a passion for the arts the way that I had been taught when I was in school. Granted, it didn't pay that well, but Beckett had his MBA. He worked for an amazing firm out of Atlanta and made a solid six figure income. We didn't need anything else.

"No, not really. It's just that we have plenty to be comfortable, but..." His words trailed off. His eyes pleaded with me to understand.

"But what?"

"But this could set us up for retirement, our children's education, you would never have to teach. You could just stay home and paint and not have to worry about whether your work will ever sell or not."

"Beckett," I whispered his name as my heart cracked wide open. "This is not okay."

"Please, Courtney. Do this for me. Do it for Flynn and his family. When it's all over, we'll have our day, and our future will be set financially so that we never have to worry about anything."

"Fine." I agreed reluctantly. If my own fiancé wasn't going to fight against this stupid plan, then why should I?

"I make plenty, but I'm already worried how we'll afford college for the three children you want to have," his argument continued when the one word I said didn't sink in right away.

"I said, *fine!*" I reiterated with a little snap in my tone.

"You – what? Oh! Shit, I didn't realize. Seriously? You'll do it?" Every word out of his mouth was said in rapid-fire succession, as if he needed to hurry before I changed my mind.

"I hope you don't regret asking me to do this." The warning sat hot on my tongue, because I already knew this would do more than put a few cracks in the shiny veneer of our relationship. This would eventually destroy us. I felt it in my bones. It was too bad that Beckett didn't seem to realize, or maybe it was just that he truly didn't care.

Chapter Two

FLYNN

I STARED at the text that had just come in over my phone. "What a moron!"

"What's that?" I turned my phone to show my sister, Bea, the text our cousin just sent me.

> Beckett: Courtney agreed. My wedding is now yours.

"Oh my God!" Bea hissed. "He did not convince his fiancée to marry you!"

"I didn't think it was possible," I mumbled. Courtney was the dream girl all men measured their future wives against. She was the type of woman who you held onto against all odds once you were lucky enough to lock her down.

Courtney was the one that you put a ring on, settled down with, and never-ever thought for a single second about stepping out on. She was sweet, understanding, willing to compromise, and when she took you into her circle of trust, the loyalty she showed was unwavering.

"He's an idiot. There's no way Courtney agreed to do this without it causing a rift between them. She's been planning their wedding for years and he just..." Bea's voice trailed off. Like me, she was probably imagining all the ways this was going to go awry.

"Should I call her?" I asked as my eyes remained glued to the stupid text.

Bea shook her head adamantly. "No. You should set up a meeting to see her in person. There are things you will both need to discuss ahead of time and..." My sister was quiet for far too long, and it worried me.

"And?" I questioned as I glanced up to see the devastation on her face. It would no doubt be a thousand times worse when if it was Courtney standing there.

"And be kind to her. She must be absolutely crushed right now."

I watched as my sister worriedly pulled her thick, curly hair back and stuffed it into one of those scrunchy things she and our other sister always left lying around everywhere. Her eyes looked a bit misty as she chewed on her bottom lip, deep in thought.

"I should call this whole thing off. I never planned to do it anyway. I only humored Beckett's wild idea because of what I overheard Dad say." Bea nodded her head before her eyes met mine.

"I know why you agreed to think about it. I heard him on the phone when I went over to see Mom and Mina."

"I wish he would confide in us about the business so we can help."

Bea laughed. "Mina is in college and I am a teacher. I'm not sure what we could do to help, but you have to know

8

that doesn't mean Dad's problems are on your shoulders, Flynn."

"I know that, but dammit," I glanced back down at the text. "I can't let this be for nothing now. Courtney didn't deserve this." My eyes met Bea's worried gaze. "She's going to hate me for this."

"No," my sister stated. "Courtney isn't stupid. She's going to focus all her anger on Beckett, where it belongs." She sighed and then patted my shoulder. "I know you used to have a thing for Courtney. I'm not sure you should do this. As much as I hate this situation for her, I think it will end up hurting you as well. I hate that Beckett chose to do this to her because she doesn't deserve it, but you're my brother and I don't want to see you hurt either."

"I think maybe I need to talk to Beckett face-to-face before I go see Courtney. Maybe I can still talk him out of this."

My sister sighed and then moved in to give me a hug. "I love that you would put her first when he won't. Don't expect too much from our cousin, Flynn. I think he's been looking for an excuse to gain his freedom without looking like the bad guy, and this opportunity seemed too good to be true."

"I don't understand why. Courtney is the goal and he already has her."

Bea shrugged her shoulders. "He also never had to work for her. They've been friends their whole lives and started dating early on, as well. It has always been a given that they would end up together. My guess is that Beckett can't appreciate what he didn't have to work for."

"That's fucking dumb," I groused. "Maybe it isn't a

good idea to go see him. My fist is itching to make contact with his face more than I want to talk sense into him."

Bea giggled. "He would probably sue you, since Grandpa didn't even mention him in his Will."

I grumbled again. "I think everyone forgot that Grandpa might not have mentioned him, or you and Mina, but he did add a stipulation that it was up to me if I chose to share what was handed to me."

"I don't want any part of it, so keep it all. I'm pretty sure Mina feels the same."

"Why?"

Bea shrugged her shoulders. "Money isn't everything. It might help, but it causes just as many problems as it resolves." My sister gave me a look that said more than her words did. "Look at what it is doing to Courtney right now."

"Somehow, I don't think that has as much to do with money as Beckett would like for everyone to think." I glanced back down at the text on my phone and re-lived the shock at seeing those words again.

> Beckett: Courtney agreed. My wedding is now yours.

I breathed out a heavy sigh and then let my fingers fly across the keyboard on my phone as I responded.

> Flynn: We need to meet up.

> Beckett: Can't. Busy at the moment.

I scrolled away from my texts and moved to FlipStack, the social media of choice for people who love putting it all out there. Sure enough, a picture had been uploaded to my cousin's page showing him at Porter's Pub. Bea leaned over and noticed what I was looking at.

"I hope Courtney hasn't seen this." We both stared down at the image of my cousin with a blonde plastered to his side and some of his buddies cheering him on in the background. "He's in full-on celebration mode."

"On second thought, I don't need to go see our cousin. I'm going to head over to Courtney's place."

"Let me know if you need backup."

"For what?"

"All the emotions," Bea whispered sadly as she grabbed her purse and got ready to leave my house.

"Hey!" I called out to her. When she turned my way, I offered a smile to my sister. "You never mentioned why you stopped by."

"I just wanted to check on you. With the wedding two weeks away, I figured you'd be stewing in all that unrequited love you had for Courtney. Your player ways never fooled me, Flynn." Bea waved her hand as she turned and left my house. I stood there and stared at the door as it closed behind my eldest sibling. Sure, she knew about my crush on my cousin's girl years ago, but I thought everyone bought the fact that I loved my single, no-strings take on dating. There had been women in and out of my life, and my bed, over the years, especially after Court and Beckett announced their engagement, but none of it had been satisfying. It was all a distraction to try to take my mind off the one woman I wished I could have. I guess I hadn't done that great a job, since my sister saw through it.

Chapter Three

COURTNEY

I swiped at my face, surprised that there weren't any tears to wipe away. Beckett left a few hours ago, and with his departure, my heart seemed to freeze over. One day, when it thawed, the tears would come. Until then, I was left to stew in a numb state of disbelief. How could he do this to me two weeks before our wedding?

A knock at the door startled me out of the loop of never-ending questions that Beckett would never answer. I couldn't get that look of satisfaction and anticipation out of my mind. He was happy to break things off and shove me off to someone else. When I finally made it to the door, my heart hammered against my chest. Part of me hoped it was my fiancé, back to say it was some awful social media prank for views on FlipStack or something. The other part of me was afraid that it might be someone else, and I would have to face my emotions. As I stood there debating between which inevitability was better, someone knocked on the door again.

I didn't even bother to look through the peephole.

Instead, I opened the door and stepped back in time to see Flynn with his hands stuffed into his pockets as his eyes raked over me. "Courtney," his voice was soft and filled with understanding as I crumbled before him. Flynn reached out and pulled me into his arms. He must have closed and locked the door, though I wasn't aware of it. Before I checked back into reality, we were already seated on my couch with me cuddled up on Flynn's lap as his hand traced soothingly up and down my back and he quietly murmured nonsense words to calm me.

"How could he?" I asked.

"I don't know," Flynn answered. "I thought he was joking when he told me he was going to ask you to do this."

"I thought he might be joking too, but then..." I cut myself off and sniffled instead of finishing.

"But then?" he encouraged me to get it all out. I leaned back and realized just how close I was. It was only then I truly registered that I was seated on Flynn's lap.

"Shit!" I jumped back off his legs and settled in beside him instead. "Beckett looked pleased with himself. I swear, Flynn, it looked like he was a kid who knew all the Christmas presents under the tree were for him and he was ready to dive in."

The lack of surprise in Flynn's eyes made me curious, morbidly so. "I'm sorry," he finally said, which only made me feel even worse. He didn't try to deny it or tell me that maybe I was imagining things. Flynn's green eyes never left mine as I tried to puzzle through it.

"You think he made this decision on purpose?"

"That much is obvious."

"Yeah, but I mean, you don't think it had as much to do

with helping you, do you? He has another reason for agreeing to do this."

"Courtney, I never asked him for this. I wouldn't do that to you."

"You didn't?"

Flynn shook his head. His dark hair was cut too short to flop around in his face the way Beckett's did when his gel gave out. Where my former fiancé had caramel-colored eyes, Flynn's were a mossy green on the outside and grew lighter the closer to his pupil you got. It was something I'd never noticed before.

"Can you explain that to me?"

"What did Beckett tell you?" he asked.

I shook my head. "No. I don't want to go into that yet. I want you to tell me how this all came to be."

Flynn heaved out a weighty sigh. "When my grandfather passed, he had a stipulation in his will that I had to be married before I was thirty if I wanted to collect the inheritance."

"You're only 26," I reminded him.

"Yes, I just turned 26. According to the terms laid out, I have been able to access my inheritance since I turned 25, but I'm not able to do that unless I'm married."

"So, why now?"

"My father's business is failing. I wanted to help him fix things, so I stupidly told Beckett about it. We were just talking about things over a few beers one night. I never meant for him to offer you up as a solution. I wouldn't do that to you. The two of you have been solid since I met you."

I nodded my head because I had thought that too, right

up until my conversation with Beckett earlier. "So, you didn't tell him you needed a wife?"

"No, I did. I told him I had to think about getting serious with someone." Flynn chuckled darkly and shook his head, as if in disbelief. "Beckett started telling me all the reasons that wouldn't work, not the least of which was that I would have to worry about gold diggers wanting to marry me for the money."

"That's when he offered me up as a solution?"

"It was later, after a few more beers," Flynn admitted. "I thought that was all it was, just a drunk man's solution to my problem. A joke. You know?" I shook my head, because no, I didn't see how offering your fiancée to someone else could ever be construed as a joke.

"So, when did it become reality?"

Flynn's shoulders tensed. "He came to see me again the next day, when I got off work. He asked about the stipulations in the will, about the cabin, and if we could make a trade." Flynn shook his head and leaned forward with his elbows on his knees as he dropped his head low into his hands and shook it back and forth. "I thought he was just trying to work through the logistics with me, so that I would think about selling him the cabin - or giving it to him." Flynn turned and made eye contact before he continued. "The minute he mentioned me becoming the groom at your wedding, I laughed at him. I swear to you, Courtney, I thought he was joking."

"He wasn't."

"No, he wasn't. He mentioned it a couple more times, and each time I blew him off and told him you would never agree to something like that. I told him it would hurt you if he even asked, and that I didn't want that. Then I got a text telling me you agreed."

"Can I see it?"

Flynn pulled his phone out, unlocked it, and pulled up his texts with my former fiancé. I felt sick when I read it, and even worse when I noticed that Flynn tried to meet up with his cousin to talk about what he had done, and Beckett blew him off.

"I came here the minute he refused to talk to me. I'm so sorry, Courtney. Please, know that I won't hold you to this. I don't know what that means for you and Beckett now, but I don't want to…"

I cut Flynn off. "No. I agreed. I will marry you, but I have my own stipulations."

"I'm afraid to ask."

I smiled at my friend and took his hand in mine. "I don't blame you, Flynn. This is all on Beckett. He is the only one responsible for ending our engagement, giving our wedding - my dream wedding - away, and putting you in this position. If you want to go through with this, I will - for you. My stipulations are as follows: Beckett does not get that cabin. If you choose to sell it, it can be to anyone but him, and you can't give it to him." Flynn's eyes widened in shock as I stated that. "Also, he mentioned that you might pay us - me - for doing this for you. I don't want any money from you. We can have a prenup drawn up if you wish. I also don't want a dime of your inheritance to go to Beckett. He chose this path, but I don't think he should profit from it in any way. If you can agree to those things, then you have yourself a wife and a wedding in two weeks."

Flynn squeezed my hands in his and offered up a pitiful

version of a smile. "I will do whatever you want, but please know that you don't have to go through with this."

I shook my head. "I planned this wedding. Everything is paid for already. I may never get married again in this life, especially after what Beckett did. Let's do this, so that I have these memories. At least my wedding will be with someone who cares enough about me to offer a real choice."

"I will have your stipulations put into a contract, so you know I won't go back on them."

"I trust you, Flynn."

"After what Beckett pulled, I am shocked you'd trust me, but I'm going to have it put in writing anyway because I have a feeling once the shock wears off, you'll need it."

"Thank you for looking out for me."

"I will always look out for you, Court."

"Why?"

"We've been friends a long time," was the answer he gave, but there was something in his eyes that spoke of something more. I didn't have the courage to ask questions though. The end of my rope had officially been reached when I realized that not only had Beckett been planning this for some time, but he had been the one to suggest it too.

Chapter Four

"What are you doing here?" I asked Beckett as I stood in the door and didn't offer him a chance to come into my place.

"I came to take you to your bachelor party."

"My bachelor party?" I asked, completely taken off guard by the thought.

"You're getting married in two days. Every man needs a bachelor party before he gets hitched."

"My marriage isn't real," I reminded my cousin.

He shrugged. "Doesn't matter. You still get a bachelor party. Besides, everyone is already waiting for us."

"Everyone?" I was confused because the way Beckett was talking, this had been something that was already arranged and I should have known about.

"Well," he hedged and then laughed. "It was supposed to be my bachelor party, but now it is yours."

"I never got an invite before." I hadn't meant to say it out loud, but since I had, it took Beckett by surprise.

"Oh, I didn't know. Maybe Grant forgot to tell you?" I

could tell he was lying. Grant, one of the assholes Beckett worked with, wouldn't have missed an opportunity to exclude me if he could. For some reason, I thought maybe I'd been left off the guest list for another reason.

"Look, I'm not really feeling a bachelor party, man. Go, enjoy without me."

"Nope. We're not taking no for an answer. Even your sister's bestie will be there to hang out with you."

"Ky is coming?" That wasn't something Ky would have done for Beckett. I didn't think they liked one another.

"Yeah. As soon as I told him that it was your bachelor party now, he said he'd be there. Maybe he's trying to get into Bea's good graces by supporting you." Beckett shrugged his shoulders.

Ky had been my older sister, Bea's, best friend for as long as I could remember. In recent years, especially while she was dating Law, we had also become a lot closer as friends. The poor sap had been in love with her for longer than he cared to admit. That meant he leaned on me when he couldn't stand to see her with another man. I felt like a bit of an asshole for not reaching out to invite him to my bachelor party. Then again, my life had taken an unexpected turn and I still hadn't fully processed everything. That included the bachelor party I now had to attend.

"I have to get dressed," I told Beckett. He pushed his way inside.

"I'll wait."

"Are you sure you still want to do this? It's not too late to back out," I called out to my cousin as I made my way to my bedroom.

"Hell no, I'm not backing out of a bachelor party."

"I meant the wedding. Me marrying Courtney, the woman who is supposed to be *your* fiancée. If you stood up and said you weren't okay with this after all, she might forgive you."

Beckett threw his head back and laughed. "Dude, you don't know Courtney as well as I do. Trust me, the girl has been in love with me since we were in first grade. There isn't a damn thing that will change the way she feels about me. This is just a momentary pause in our life-long relationship."

"I don't think she sees it that way." I glared over at the idiot before I ripped my t-shirt over my head and grabbed a nicer button-up shirt out of my closet.

"She's a little miffed that her 'dream wedding' was hijacked and that it will have to be different when we eventually get married. Courtney will get over that and come up with an even better theme for our wedding." I wanted to punch him for the way he put the words 'dream wedding' in air quotes, as if it was a trivial thing.

He sounded so confident, but the asshole hadn't seen the way she broke down over what he'd done. The poor thing hadn't even realized she was in my lap when I sat on the couch with her in my arms a couple weeks ago. Courtney was having a hard time wrapping her mind around the situation, not that anyone could blame her. It wasn't every day that the man you were supposed to marry offered you up to someone else instead. Part of me still wanted to call everything off, but Courtney needed to go through with it. I was certain that she wanted to see if Beckett would eventually step up and stop it from happening. Unfortunately, for her, I didn't think that was going to happen. My cousin seemed pretty eager to get to my bachelor party, and I could only imagine why.

I WAS SHOCKED that the bachelor party wasn't being thrown in some downtown Atlanta strip club. Instead, we went to a bar closer to home that most of us frequented when we wanted to go out. In all honesty, that should have been my first indication that things would go to shit by the end of the night.

"Hey man," Ky, my sister's best friend, said as he clapped me on the back. "This is weird, right? It's not just me?"

I chuckled in response. "No, man, it is definitely not just you. I had no clue this was even going down until Beckett showed up at my door."

Ky stepped back and looked shocked. "What the fuck is he thinking?"

"No clue. He ruined a good woman, though. Courtney is holding it together, but she's heartbroken."

"I can see that. It's a complete betrayal. This was supposed to be their wedding, and that asshole has been in the bar for five minutes and he has a woman in his lap." I turned to see where Ky pointed his beer bottle.

"You have got to be kidding me," I growled before I glanced around to see who else was in the bar who might eventually make sure the news got back to Courtney.

"You had to know. Bea told me you suspected that he had a wandering eye months ago."

"I didn't think it would go further than that." It made

me wonder if that was why he pushed for her to marry me instead. The asshole had cold feet and wanted it to look like there was another, more noble, reason for backing out of their wedding.

Ky and I watched in complete disgust as my cousin and the woman sucked face. It was obvious, by their comfort level, that this was not their first time together.

"That's not hard to watch at all." I spun at the sound of her voice and turned to see Courtney there with my sister, Bea.

"Ky told me where he was going and why," Bea said automatically as she threw her hands up in surrender.

"I made her bring me here. I needed to see for myself."

Just as I was about to usher my future wife and my sister out of the bar, we heard a woman shriek. I turned to see the woman Beckett had been making out with scream as another woman yanked her off his lap by her hair. "You crawled out of my bed this morning and now you have some skank in your lap at the bar for everyone to see?" the second woman yelled at him. His eyes lifted and searched the area, maybe in an effort to find someone to help him out of his situation. When they landed on me, he looked relieved until he noticed who was with me. What color was left in his face drained as he realized Courtney was there to witness everything.

"It's not what it looks like," he shouted to her.

"Who in the hell are you talking to?" The second woman yelled as she followed the direction of Beckett's eyes. The minute she noticed Courtney, she growled. I took that to mean she knew exactly who Beckett's former fiancée was. "You told me you were done with that bitch."

That got Beckett's attention. "Don't talk about her like that."

"Screw you, Beckett Robeson! You made promises to me that you wouldn't go through with the wedding. I thought I could trust you when everyone started to talk about how she was going to marry your cousin instead, but then I found you here with someone else."

"Oh shit," Ky muttered.

Courtney stomped closer to them, despite me trying to grab for her, so I could get us all out of the club and spare her more hurt. "Just how long have you been screwing Beckett, Ashley?" she asked the woman.

The woman, Ashley apparently, turned and grinned. "For a month."

"A month?" Courtney whispered, but the bar had gone so quiet that we all managed to hear it. Courtney turned to Beckett and repeated the two words louder. "A month, Beckett?"

"We weren't screwing for a month. We were talking and then after…"

"You were talking about screwing her and didn't bother to go through with it until you dumped me onto your cousin?" Courtney asked. Beckett didn't even bother to answer besides the slight nod of his head.

"Good to know."

"I swear, nothing happened before," he hurriedly explained again.

"He's not lying about that," Ashley confirmed as she threw a shitty look his way.

"You hadn't done anything, but you talked about it,

made a plan, and then followed through the minute you passed me off to be someone else's problem."

"It's not like that," Beckett argued.

"It was exactly like that," Ashley taunted.

"Okay, that's enough!" I growled at her as I pulled Courtney back away from them.

"What the fuck were you thinking telling her to come here?" Beckett asked me.

"I didn't. I wouldn't have wanted her to see that shit, even if I had known you were going to publicly start dating other people instead of waiting."

"What did you think would happen? You marry my fiancée and I sit around waiting until the day you can divorce her?" He scoffed. "I have needs."

"Funny thing about needs, Beckett," Courtney taunted him. "I have them too."

"What?" he asked, and for the second time that night, I watched as the color drained from his face.

"You heard me. I have needs, and I'll be married, so I guess it will be okay for me to see to those needs with my husband." Courtney grabbed my arm and pulled me back further as I watched my cousin's face transform with rage.

"He won't fucking touch you!" Beckett demanded.

"Fuck you, Beckett Robeson! You're going to stand there and pretend that you have a right to say anything to me? YOU CHEATED!" Courtney called out as we turned to leave the bar.

"No, I didn't."

"We never broke up, so if you slept with her, that means you cheated on me." Beckett opened his mouth to argue the point and then closed it. This happened several times in a row and made him look like a fish trying to breathe out of water. "I have loved you literally my whole life and you couldn't wait to get rid of me."

"No, that's not true!" He tried to deny it, but the truth was staring us all in the face. He had pushed Courtney off on me to marry, but they had never officially broken up. "I didn't realize you thought we were still together," the asshole had the nerve to say.

"Why the hell would I think we were broken up when you were telling me we would still get married and that you'd have the cabin and the money to help pay for our three children's college funds?"

"Shit," Beckett huffed out as Courtney continued out the door without another word.

Chapter Five

COURTNEY

"I'm so sorry. I don't know what I was thinking. Beckett is your cousin. He'll hate you for the way I just taunted him."

Bea scoffed out a half laugh at my pseudo apology.

"No offense, Courtney, but Beckett only has himself to blame for this whole situation. Seems to me, after what we just heard, that he was looking for any excuse. He might not have cheated physically, but he was already planning to before he pushed you off on Flynn. If you had refused and gone through with the wedding to him, he would have cheated or called it off."

"Why? I don't understand. I have dedicated my whole life to loving that man, and he behaved like he couldn't wait to get rid of me." Flynn pulled me into his arms and held me there as I cried in the parking lot.

"Let's get you out of here," he murmured in my ear. "You don't need all the busybodies to see you break down over my asshole cousin."

"We'll follow you," Bea stated as she handed her car keys to Flynn. "I assume the asshat brought you here."

When Flynn nodded and took her keys, she told him, "I'll ride with Ky."

Flynn helped me into Bea's passenger seat and then moved around the car to get in on the other side. I stared at the door of the bar. He didn't even bother to come out and check on me, to follow us, to deny anything, to try to make things right. Beckett didn't bother to fight for me. He was too busy with the two - TWO - women he had fighting over him in the bar. My heart hammered in my chest as I thought about the fact that he had started talking to at least one of them before he offered me up to marry another man. Even when he did that, I didn't think it meant we were broken up. I thought it meant that our marriage was on hold, not our relationship. That's what I got for thinking instead of questioning everything, I supposed.

"I know this is a dumb question, but I feel like I have to ask anyway, are you okay?"

I turned to see Flynn's concerned eyes on me. I offered him a hint of smile before I dropped my eyes to where my hands rested on my lap. "No. I don't know if I'll ever be okay after this. I thought it was just about the money and that stupid cabin. Turns out, it was about him seeing other people all along."

"I'm guessing by what you said back there that he never even bothered to actually break it off with you."

"No, he didn't. I honestly thought this," I waved my hand back and forth between us, "was all for show and that he and I were still a couple." I swiped a hand down my face, as if I could wipe everything I saw from my mind. That was impossible. "I don't know why I thought that."

"Because he never told you otherwise. I think any sane

person would have assumed that nothing changed about your relationship."

"Any sane person wouldn't have offered me up to marry his cousin for money that we didn't need."

"Well, this is Beckett we're talking about," Flynn teased. "Sorry, not the time for jokes."

"No, it is because everything feels like a bad joke, only someone forgot to tell me the punchline so I can laugh about it."

We were quiet for most of the ride back to his house. It was only when we pulled into his driveway that I realized that was where we had been headed the whole time. "I thought you were taking me home?"

Flynn shrugged his shoulders as he got out of the car. Once he was at my door, he opened it and held his hand out to me. I took it, despite being confused about why we were there. "My cousin has a key to your place, right?"

"Yes."

"I thought you might want to be somewhere he couldn't get into easily, at least for the night."

"Thanks, I hadn't thought about that." I didn't bother to add the fact that I didn't think Beckett cared enough about me to come to my house anyway. He was too busy juggling his other women to care about how heartbroken I was. My house was actually a guest cottage on my parents' property. When they bought the place, the cottage was originally supposed to be my mom's art studio, since she was a painter and sculptor too. Unfortunately, arthritis and other health issues hit her too hard to continue. When I came home from college, my parents offered the cottage to me, so that I could save for my wedding, honeymoon, and a home that Beckett and I could start a family in.

They had even suggested that they would be okay with Beckett moving in too, so that he could also save for those things. My parents were very traditional, so to make that concession had been a stretch for them. Beckett declined their offer, saying he wanted to do everything with me the right way. It made my parents respect him more. In hindsight, it made me wonder how long he had been plotting his freedom. Why couldn't he have spoken up sooner? It would have saved me a ton of money on a wedding. Even if I wanted to help Flynn out, we could have had a quickie marriage at the Justice of the Peace and been done with it for less than two hundred dollars.

I followed Flynn into his house. It was a beautiful space with a huge backyard and a sunroom to die for. As an artist, I could spend all day in that room, or out in the yard, painting. I wasn't sure why he chose the house, since he had been a serious bachelor as long as I'd known him, and his house was made for a family. In fact, when Beckett and I discussed what kind of home we wanted to buy in our future, I told him I wanted one exactly like Flynn's.

"I've always loved it here," I murmured.

"Yeah?" Flynn asked as he turned to close and lock the door behind us.

"It's the perfect home to raise a family." I blushed profusely as I realized that it might sound like more than what I meant.

"That's why I bought it."

I turned to look at him. "I don't understand. You haven't even dated anyone seriously."

"No, I haven't. That doesn't mean I didn't think about my future when I bought this place. I wanted a nice piece of property and a good home for whenever the time came to be serious."

"And you don't think your future wife and mother of your children will care that it was once the bachelor pad you brought all your women to?" I asked and immediately wished I wouldn't have when the tips of Flynn's ears turned red and he ducked his head in what could only be embarrassment.

"I guess I hadn't thought about that," he mumbled.

"I'm sorry. I have no room to judge anyone. I'm marrying my former fiancé's cousin. At this point, I'm doing it to spite him. I'm sure one day, if I ever date again, I'll have to explain that, and Lord knows, I'll sound like a crazy woman." I chuckled. "Maybe we'll need to stay married to one another, Flynn. I'm not sure anyone else would have us." I winked at him to let him know I was kidding, but his grin said something different. Again, I wasn't in the right frame of mind to think too deeply on it until he spoke.

"I don't think that would be a bad thing, Court."

"Oh!" It was the only response I was capable of as Flynn's ears burned hot again before he turned to head to his kitchen. I followed behind as my brain tried to process and finally gave up because I was too overwhelmed to consider living a life with my former fiancé's cousin.

"Can I get you anything?" Flynn offered.

"I'll take water."

Flynn's brows rose in question, or maybe shock, as he turned to grab a glass out of the cabinet. "Figured you would want something stronger after the bar."

I shook my head. "Nope. If I hit the strong stuff, I'm not sure I'd come back up for a while and I need to be sober to marry you this weekend."

Flynn put the glass down on the counter and moved to stand in front of me. "Courtney, I appreciate your willingness to do this, even if you thought you wouldn't have to follow through. I won't hold you to it, though. I would never force you to marry me."

"You aren't forcing me."

"No, but I'd rather your only reason for doing this not be to spite Beckett."

"You don't think he deserves it?"

"Oh, no. I think he deserves far worse, because it won't hurt him until much later. He thinks you're safe with me."

"Aren't I?"

Flynn leaned in closer and the smile that spread across his face was nearly my undoing. "You will always be safe with me, Courtney, but the safety Beckett is thinking about is entirely different."

"What do you mean?" I managed to choke past my suddenly dry throat.

"He thinks you're safe from me wanting you, from pushing physical boundaries only he thinks should remain in place."

"And you don't see it like that?"

He shook his head slowly from side to side. "Nope."

"Nope," I whispered, though I wasn't sure if it was a question or what.

"Nope. I don't see it like that at all. If you marry me, and you give me even the tiniest hint that you might be interested in more than a marriage in name only, there's not a damn thing to stop me from having more with you." He leaned in a little further and placed a quick kiss on my cheek, but it was close enough that he caught the corner of my mouth too. His green eyes twinkled in delight at my shocked expression as he pulled back. Then, before I could read anything into the situation, he turned and moved back to the glass he placed on the counter. He filled the damn thing up, as if he hadn't left me standing there in a Flynn Fog and handed it to me. His steady hand made my quivering one seem to shake harder.

Could I go there with Flynn?

I wasn't sure if it was a smart idea, but the zing of electric energy between us made me think maybe it wasn't completely out of the realm of possibility. Then again, that could have been my spiteful need for revenge rearing its ugly head. Flynn was right, Beckett assumed I was safe with his cousin. I was beginning to think he might have been wrong.

Chapter Six

FLYNN

I stood in the room that had been set aside for the groom to prepare for the wedding, and it felt as though the fires of hell itself were responsible for heating the place. "Is anyone else sweating?" I asked.

My father's immediate response was to mockingly laugh at me. "It's okay to have cold feet, Son."

"I wish my feet were cold," I grumbled. "I'm about to sweat my balls off in here." Dad wasn't fooling anyone. Sweat beaded up on his forehead too.

"I'll go check and make sure the guests aren't making puddles in the church," Ky, my eldest sister's husband and my best man, announced as he quickly launched himself from the room. I didn't blame him. None of us wanted to sit in a sauna in a tuxedo.

The minute he left, I turned to see if I could open one of the windows. By the time I managed to get it cracked open, a familiar sparkling metallic silver BMW pulled into the Handicap space just to the right of the window. I rolled my eyes at my cousin's audacity as my stomach plummeted knowing that Courtney would either not be happy to see him there or would ride off into the sunset with the jerk and leave me hanging at the altar like an idiot.

The odds of the latter happening diminished quickly as a giggling blonde, who looked like she was dressed for a night of clubbing instead of a wedding, wobbled out of the car without any assistance from Beckett. My eyes landed on my cousin again and I noticed he wore a tuxedo, though rumpled to shit, instead of a suit as other wedding guests would. I hoped like hell he didn't think he would be able to slide back into the wedding as the groom. Then again, I wouldn't put anything past him.

"This is not happening!" I growled as his smug gaze met mine through the window. My father came over to see what had me so concerned, and as soon as he noticed Beckett, he swore under his breath.

"I'll handle this. It is almost time. Get yourself down that aisle to wait for your bride. I have a feeling Courtney will one day thank her lucky stars that she married you and not my idiot nephew."

He was gone before I could respond. What could I say, though? I hoped so, because I had been a little bit in love with my soon-to-be wife since I first met her in middle school. Considering this was more of an arranged marriage for convenience, admitting my real feelings felt like the wrong thing to do. Did it make me a creep to end up with the woman who I secretly loved when she didn't know? I wasn't sure, but I refused to take a chance on telling her, in case it made her want to run away.

"Everyone is about ready, and this room is the only inferno in the place." I turned to see Ky in the doorway. He had come back to fill me in. It made me wonder if my path to hell was already paved in flames, considering the room I was supposed to wait in was like standing in one of its infamous pits.

"Am I doing the right thing?" I asked him. There was a time, not too long ago, when he had been the swapped groom in a wedding. He did it to save my sister the embarrassment of being left at the altar, but the sad sack was also hopelessly in love with her too.

"She knew what she agreed to. If it makes you feel better, everyone thinks she traded up to the better cousin."

It didn't really make me feel better to be a last-minute trade-up, especially since it hadn't been her idea to do it. Still, I huffed out a quick breath full of anxiety, squared my shoulders, and marched to the door. "Let's do this."

Chapter Seven

COURTNEY

"AM I REALLY DOING THIS?" I whispered to my reflection in the mirror.

My makeup was perfect, done in soft tones that matched the silver and peach theme I'd finally chosen for the wedding. I looked like the perfect bride. Most of my hair was swept up into an intricate updo while some of it escaped to frame my face with soft russet curls. My eyes stood out in stark contrast to everything, because the panic in them was evident. How could I marry a different man than the one I planned this wedding with? My heartbeat tripped around in my chest, a chaotic beat that mirrored my conflicting emotions.

Part of me wanted to march down that aisle and proclaim my undying loyalty to Flynn simply to spite Beckett. Another part of me wanted to rip the wedding dress from my body and burn it along with all the decorations. Fuck the Robeson family. I was angry and that frustration needed a release that I wasn't sure I was capable of. The final part of me wanted to slink off in my dress and go have a cry all by my lonesome. I needed to cry for the future that we had planned for years and was now lost because Beckett wanted me to marry someone else. After I saw him at what should have been his bachelor party, it became clear that Flynn's problem wasn't the only reason my fiancé wanted me to agree to this farce of a marriage.

He wanted out.

Even if it was only temporarily, my fiancé wanted to go explore things with other women. I couldn't even fathom wanting to be with someone other than Beckett. It had been the two of us against the world for our whole lives. At least, that was what I had always believed. My eyes were opened and with my new understanding came the dreaded hindsight. The rose-colored glasses had come off and I was able to see all the red flags in our relationship that I had explained away and failed to take heed of. My relationship had been doomed long before Beckett suggested that I help out his cousin by marrying Flynn temporarily.

My eyes drifted down my body in the mirror again. My dress fit perfectly with a gorgeous corset top that puffed out into a ballgown style dress from the waist down. It had been my dream dress for years. I'd saved babysitting money, waitressing tips, and eventually part of my salary every month to get the dress of my dreams. There was no question that I didn't want to compromise on this, so I refused to allow anyone to help me pay for the dress.

I had been so careful with my plan too. I wasn't normally a superstitious person, but I made sure that Beckett never knew what my dress would look like. He used to laugh and tell me that it was ridiculous. It wasn't something I was willing to compromise on, though. I wanted the first time he saw me in the perfect wedding dress to be the minute I walked down that aisle to pledge my life and love to him. That would never happen.

This would all be for Flynn.

My heart tripped up on the next beat as I thought about the man who was at the center of this whole damn thing, even if he wasn't to be blamed for the circumstances I found myself in. Flynn had been a good friend since middle school. If I had never known Beckett, if we hadn't grown up together before Flynn came on the scene, I might have fallen for him instead. There was a time when we were in high school that I had been confused and almost left Beckett. The only thing that stopped me then was knowing how weird everything would be if I went from one cousin to the other. Our families were so closely interwoven that it felt like it would have been a betrayal to go there, and I never wanted to come between the bond Flynn had with Beckett.

I got over whatever made me angry enough with Beckett back then to set my sights on Flynn, and I never allowed my mind to drift back there. It was ironic that I stood there, staring at myself in my wedding gown, while the two men at the center of my world swapped places as the groom in my wedding.

A knock on the door pulled me out of my reverie. I turned to see my dad as he peeked his head around the door. The stunned look on his face told me that I wasn't wrong about the dress. "Courtney," he whispered before he quickly made his way into the room and shut the door. "You look like a princess, sweetheart." His usually stoic eyes misted over, and my stomach dropped as my nose burned from holding back tears.

"Daddy," I whispered and before I could even register the movement, I was in his strong embrace.

"We can leave right now. No man deserves to see you like this unless he is ready to pledge himself to you forever. All of your beauty - inside and out - shouldn't be for a man who doesn't deserve it."

"Flynn isn't the man who doesn't deserve it, Dad."

"What do you mean?"

I hadn't told my parents about the latest developments in my relationship with Beckett. I sighed and let the tension drain away from my shoulders as I released my father from our hug. Then I explained what I'd found out during the bachelor party and how Flynn told me that he wouldn't hold me to this arrangement.

"Maybe he is the only man who deserves to see you like this," my dad stated. "Never thought I'd want to punch Beckett in the nuts more than the time I walked in on the two of you."

A red-hot blush stained my cheeks as I remembered how disastrously my first time with Beckett had gone. We had been fifteen at the time and my parents came home early from an evening out, thanks to one of my mother's many migraines. My dad came up to check on me and found Beckett mid thrust as my legs snaked around his hips. It was still, to date, the most embarrassing moment of my life.

My father cleared his throat, obviously just as embarrassed that he brought that moment in time up. "I will smuggle you out of here right now, if that's what you want, and your mother and I will make sure that the cost of this wedding doesn't fall on your shoulders."

"Thank you, I appreciate that. I'm not going to waste

this dress, the wedding I worked so hard to plan, and Flynn doesn't deserve to be disappointed."

"You don't owe him anything," Dad reminded me.

"No, I don't, but at this point, if the best thing that comes out of this whole mess is my ability to help a friend and his family, I am going to do that."

Dad must have seen something in my eyes because he chuckled and pulled me into another hug. "Plus, it will be fun to rub it in Beckett's face. When he sees what should have been his bride looking this stunning as she says, 'I do' to another man, it is going to hit him hard."

"I didn't say there weren't any perks for me."

"Come on, then. I'm sure Flynn is waiting anxiously to see if you'll go through with this."

"You don't think Beckett will show up today, do you?" I asked as my father guided me out of the room I used to get ready.

"Probably not, but if he does, I'm glad I'll be there to witness his reaction."

"I truly hope he doesn't have one."

"If he's here, I promise you that he will, sweetheart."

AS I WALKED down the aisle, arm-in-arm with my dad, my eyes stayed trained on Flynn. His face was the reaction I always hoped to see from Beckett on this day. He was in awe of me as I walked toward him. There was no rationalizing how that made me feel. Everything inside me buzzed with excited energy while my body tingled in anticipation of what we were about to do. That look - the one I had always hoped to see on my wedding day - propelled me down to the altar without even a side glance at anyone who came to witness our union.

As soon as my father gave me away and placed my hand into Flynn's, my eyes lifted from our joined hands to meet his. "You are the most beautiful woman I have ever seen, Courtney." The sweetest smile spread across my face as his words took root somewhere deep in my soul. "I'm a lucky man."

I didn't think anyone heard him, but then my mom's gasp made its way to my ears and for the first time, I glanced over at the audience. She swiped a tear away and gave me an encouraging nod. It was not what I expected. She had thrown a fit when I first broke the news that it wouldn't be Beckett getting married to me, but his cousin. She had lost her shit completely. My dad hadn't had the time to tell her what I said, so I had to wonder why she suddenly had a change of heart. I half expected her to interrupt and say she objected.

Flynn reached over, ever so gently, and used his finger under my chin to guide my attention back to him. "Stay with me," he whispered lower than before to ensure I was the only one who heard him that time.

"I am," I whispered back.

"Dearly beloved, we are gathered here today to celebrate the union of Flynn Zachary Robeson and Courtney Elise Parker. If any here object to this union, let them speak now or forever hold their peace."

Gasps rang out around the room and both Flynn and I turned to see why. Beckett stood up, and a woman in a barely-there red dress stood up a moment after him. "Sit down!" he hissed at her before he turned his attention back to Flynn and me. "Courtney, don't do this. I was wrong."

He had some freaking nerve.

"I'm the one who is supposed to be up there with you!"

I couldn't help my response. I laughed at him. He seemed taken aback and about to argue his point until his date stood again and smacked him across the face. "You spent the night screwing me, and then brought me to this wedding only to ask the bride to marry you? What a fucking jerk! You leveled up, lady!" she called as she tried to push past the others in the pew to get out to the aisle. "Sorry," she insisted as she went, ass or boobs in people's faces as she did. "I'm so sorry," she whimpered before finally breaking free into the aisle. It was clear she was embarrassed. I would have felt worse if she hadn't come to someone's wedding dressed like she was ready for a night out instead of an elegant event. Then again, I was certain that was Beckett's fault too.

"Dad," I hissed.

His head snapped around to me and he gave me a nod. "I'll take care of it." He immediately moved to grab Beckett and escort him out.

"You know it's supposed to be me! Everyone here does!" Beckett shouted as my father grabbed his arm.

"You gave her up. This is your fault and now you have to live with it, but what you're not going to do is ruin my daughter's day anymore than you already have, you little asshole."

There were a few more gasps at my father's rather polite choice words for my former fiancé. As soon as Dad got him to the back of the church, a few other men stepped forward and took over to escort him out so that my father could come back to his seat.

"Sorry, folks. We can resume," Dad called out to the minister.

"Well, yes, okay then..." The Minister stumbled over himself as he tried to get back into the swing of things. I turned and stared up into Flynn's eyes and whispered, "Sorry."

He shook his head in a subtle way and offered me a closed-lip smile before we both turned back to the minister and followed along with his blessings before we recited our vows to one another.

When we got to the part where Flynn had to kiss me, I held my breath, wondering if he would do it or settle for some weird cheek kiss. I didn't have long to wait for the answer. He reached over and took my face between the palms of his hands and leaned in as he pulled me closer. "Gonna do this the right way, Court." I gave a quick nod and then his mouth was on mine. My eyes drifted closed as his lips explored mine. I was lost in the sweet kiss and the feel of his warmth transferring to me as he moved another step closer. We both opened up to deepen the kiss. Just as our tongues met, raucous cheers lifted throughout the church and rang even louder than should be expected because of the echo effect in the sanctuary.

Slowly, reluctantly, we pulled apart, but our eyes met one another's as we stood there and allowed ourselves to feel the full impact of the moment we became man and wife. The minister's proclamation was lost on us - or at least on me - as we stared at one another, still locked in an embrace with my arms on his chest and his hands cradled around my face.

"Flynn," I whispered his name as another round of cheers went up. We both turned our heads and smiled at everyone who chose to celebrate with us instead of being weird about the unexpected circumstances surrounding our wedding. After his sister Bea and her husband Ky got married in an unexpected groom swap, I guess this was no big deal to most of the guests.

"Come on, Mrs. Robeson, that's our cue to get out of here." Flynn's hand traveled down to take hold of mine and we walked hand-in-hand down the aisle as everyone showered us in peach rose petals as we walked by. My heart felt so light, I couldn't help my giggle as the petals tickled my face and shoulders. Flynn looked over and grinned at me. "So damn beautiful," he said before his hand squeezed down on mine a little to let me know that those words were all for me and not the spectacle around us.

Chapter Eight

FLYNN

HOLY SHIT!

Courtney was the most beautiful bride to ever walk down an aisle. I would stake my life on that, and I was the lucky bastard she said her vows to. It might have been by arrangement, by default, and only because my cousin was too stupid to realize exactly what a treasure he had in her; but I meant my vows. If she would let me, I'd be there for her through good times and bad, through sickness and health, and all the other promises we made to one another.

When we made it out the church doors, the sun shone in a brilliant blue sky just for us. I guess the temporary light blindness was the only reason I didn't realize Beckett was lying in wait for us. I found out real quick when he sucker-punched me. The minute he attacked, I tugged Courtney behind me to protect her.

"Don't fucking try to hide my fiancée from me!" my asshole cousin shouted.

"She's my wife, and I will protect her from harm - even if that means sheltering her from you." That made him stop in his tracks, with his fist cocked back to have another go at me. "You set this in motion," I reminded him.

"I came here today to set that right," he argued.

I scoffed, but it was Courtney who spoke. "I hate to break it to you, Beckett, but the minute I realized you set this up so that you could be with other women, the possibility of us ever getting back together came to an end."

"That's not true!"

He didn't get to argue any further because my dad, Courtney's father, Ky, and a few other men stepped up to put a wall of bodies between Beckett and my wife and me. "Come on, Court. If you don't have anything else to say to him, I'll get you out of here."

"I don't." Her insistence was sharp as I guided her down to the limo that waited for us. I opened the door and helped to get her and all the material from her dress into the car before I got in. "I guess the dress was made to be walked in and not to be stuffed into a car," Courtney tried to joke.

I smirked in her direction as I shut the door. "I'll spend the time to tuck you in properly because it was worth the effort to see you walk down that aisle looking like a fucking queen. My queen."

"Flynn," she whispered.

"I know you didn't marry me because you love me, but that doesn't mean I won't take my vows seriously, Court. I need you to know that. As long as you want this, tolerate it, or whatever it is you're doing, I will treat you exactly like the queen you are."

"And what happens when you get tired of playing happily married couple with me?" she asked. Immediately she started to nibble on her bottom lip, something she had always done when she was nervous.

"That won't be a problem."

"It could be. This was a convenience for you."

I shook my head. "Courtney, if you hadn't happily been my cousin's woman all this time, I would have made you mine a long time ago. This is anything but convenient for me. I've always wanted you and lived with the knowledge that I'd always come in second to my cousin where you were concerned."

I could tell by the look on her face that she remembered the one time we almost tried to make it work between us. It had been back in high school, in our junior year. She and Beckett had been on the outs for a while. It was another case of wandering eye for him, though I don't think she ever knew the truth of what he was up to back then. If she did, I don't see how she could have gone back to him. She had done so, though, much to my dismay.

"Are you feeling up to the reception, or did you want to skip it?" I asked after she remained quiet for so long the silence started to feel uncomfortable.

"We need to go to the reception," she said. It took a moment, but her eyes finally found mine. "I want to go to the reception with my husband and celebrate with our families. No matter how we got to this place, we're here now and I won't let anything take these memories from us. Maybe one day, we'll look back together on fond memories. Maybe, this will just be a fleeting footnote in our lives." She shrugged her shoulders. "No matter how it turns out, I want to be present in the now and not worried about a future we can't predict."

I knew there was something wrong with the way she answered because Courtney was a planner. She was always worried about the future and planning for everything. The fact that she was willing to give up that control made me ache for her in a way I couldn't describe. I knew it had to be because today she truly lost the future she had been planning so long with my cousin. I wasn't stupid enough not to realize the reason for her response. That didn't mean it had to sit well with me, though.

"Whatever you want and need, Court."

She shook her head and reached up to touch my cheek. "No. It's not just about me, Flynn. We're a team now. So, whatever we both need should be our priority."

It wasn't a declaration of undying love from her, not that I expected it, but I would take it for now.

Chapter Nine

COURTNEY

I WASN'T ready to acknowledge the zing of excitement that shot through me as I touched Flynn's face in the limo. What I told him wasn't a lie. We were a team now, for better or worse, in accordance with our vows. Despite how easily Beckett thought that could be transferred to another person, I believed in standing by my promises and that included my wedding vows. Even if he hadn't been running around with other women, I would never forsake the vows I took with Flynn to go back to Beckett. I wasn't sure if Flynn was in the right place to hear that though. He was just as much a victim of circumstance in this as I was.

"Are you ready to do this?" Flynn asked as the limo pulled up to the reception hall.

"Yes," I whispered as he took my hand in his. The warmth was a welcome balm to my nerves. "Is it weird that I'm more nervous about the reception than I was about the wedding?" I turned to see Flynn's grinning face beaming down at me.

"Not at all. I think we can quell some of those jitters though. Smash cake or no?"

"Definitely not." I pointed at my dress. "We are not ruining this masterpiece."

"On that we agree. Okay, we'll feed each other in the least messy way possible." The man winked at me and all I could offer back in response was a giggle. A freakin' giggle. Come on… He seemed pleased with that, though, so he nodded and gave my hand a reassuring squeeze. "I have a song picked out for us to dance to, but we can change it, if you'd like."

"What is it?"

"Is it okay if it remains a surprise? Do you trust me with that?"

I thought about it for a minute. If Beckett asked me that same question, my answer would have been absolutely not. There was no telling what he would have picked. For some reason, I trusted Flynn to remain classy about things. "I trust you with it."

He let out a breath and smiled at me again. "You won't be disappointed, I promise."

"I believe you." We were lost in a sweet, secret stare-off when the door to the limo opened and the driver reached his hand in to offer me help out. I took it and then looked back over my shoulder one more time at my new husband. "Whatever else happens tonight, I need you to know that I feel like we did the right thing today."

"Then I will make sure you never regret it."

FLYNN and I made our way to the penthouse suite, which he rented out for our first night together, while all of our guests made their way from the church to the hotel where the reception was being held in one of their ballrooms. "Do you need help changing into a different dress?" my new husband asked me, and then his cheeks burned red. "I can call down for your mom or my sister or someone else, if you aren't comfortable…"

I chuckled and shook my head. "I only need your help, if you don't mind."

"I don't mind." His cheeks reddened further as he realized how into helping me he sounded. "Sorry," Flynn huffed. "I know this must be a little awkward."

"Not at all." I pointed to the ballgown portion of my dress. "This puffy part comes off, but there are little buttons holding it in place all around my waistline. If you can help me with the ones in the back, I'll be ready in no time."

"Sure." Flynn was careful not to step on my dress as he moved around just over my right shoulder and searched for the first button to release it. Once we managed to get all of them unbuttoned, the skirt portion of my gown drooped away from my body just a bit. I glanced around and laughed as I saw how far I had positioned us away from any furniture.

"I really should have thought this through a bit more. If we were close to the bed, I could climb up onto it to get out of this."

"How did you get it on?"

"It was lifted over my head before the makeup and hair were done." I bit my bottom lip as I tried to think of how to do this without trampling on part of my gown, since I hoped to preserve it.

"Put your arms around my neck and hold on tight," Flynn demanded. I followed his instructions without questioning him. As soon as I had a secure hold on my husband, he reached down into the skirt that billowed away from my body and managed to wrap an arm around my legs. As he took a step back, my body pulled free from the oversized skirt, and he carried me a few steps away before he set me down again.

"Thank you," I whispered.

"Anything for my wife," he teased.

"Careful, I might hold you to that."

"Please do." The way his voice dropped on those two simple words made goosebumps erupt all over my body. How was I this attracted to the man I married, when I would have sworn I was completely in love with his cousin only a few weeks ago?

"We should get down to our reception before people start making up stories about what's taking us so long," Flynn suggested.

"Lead the way," I called out, but my husband shook his head and pulled my hand into his.

"We go together." He dropped my hand once I was beside him and wrapped his arm around me. "I'm not sure which version of your dress I like more. The big skirt made you look like Cinderella attending a ball, but this version makes you look like a sexy siren ready to lure men into your clutches."

"Thank you?" It came out as a question because I wasn't sure if being compared to an evil siren was a good thing.

"It was definitely a compliment, Court."

I grinned at him. "I'm glad you like it." Without the ball gown, it looked as though I was still wearing the corset top, but the skirt portion only flared a little at my hips and the material that covered my legs, all the way to the floor, was a white gossamer material. Beneath that was a thin satin sheath that only came mid-thigh, so all the places that needed to be covered were done so in an elegant manner. When I moved, the material swooshed around and gave the appearance that I floated everywhere. Every aspect of my wedding gown had been chosen because I wanted my wedding day to feel magical.

"I can't wait to dance with you, but I really can't wait to see the video of it. It will look like I was dancing with a goddess," Flynn remarked. It was my turn to blush profusely.

"I never knew you were such a romantic," I mentioned.

He shrugged his shoulders, but didn't bother to respond. The elevator we had taken to the second floor ballroom opened and we managed to get all the way to the ballroom doors before anyone spotted us.

"Attention everyone!" Ky announced when he saw us. "Allow me to introduce to you, Mr. and Mrs. Flynn Robeson!"

Everyone stood and cheered as Flynn swooped me up into a bridal hold and carried me over the threshold to our reception. When he set me back down on my feet, he leaned in and stole a kiss that left me breathless. I couldn't take my eyes off the man and for the life of me, I couldn't figure out why he had such an impact on my emotions.

By the time our first dance was announced, I was on

pins and needles waiting to see what song played for us. To my complete shock, it was the song I had originally wanted to dance to, but the one thing Beckett refused to have because he thought it was too depressing.

My new husband held out his hand to me and I joined mine with his as he pulled me close during the first couple notes of One Day Less by Anson Seabra. I might not have been dancing with the man I always imagined, but it was no less magical. In fact, I think the fact that it was Flynn made it better somehow. He understood me in a way Beckett never had. It was something that I never realized until Beckett's selfishness couldn't be ignored or excused away anymore.

Chapter Ten

FLYNN

"Smash it! Smash it!"

I rolled my eyes as Courtney and I cut the first piece of our wedding cake together. She had the cake picked out long before we knew we were getting married, so whatever flavor it was would be a surprise to me. Good thing I wasn't picky as fuck about food. Then again, Court had impeccable taste. It was almost as if she planned the wedding for us specifically because she had chosen some of my favorites for dinner.

"Smash it! Smash it!" A few assholes in the crowd chanted again, as if this was some fucking kegger in college and not a fucking classy wedding reception. I had no doubt those were friends of my cousin.

We each took a piece and then twined our arms. It killed me to see the trepidation there in Court's eyes. Had she married Beckett, she would have been right to assume he would take their advice and smash the cake in her face, despite the promise not to. Then again, I couldn't see the asshole respecting her enough to agree not to do it in the first place.

Very gently, I moved the piece of cake until it just touched her pretty, peach lips. Her relieved smile was everything as she opened up and took a nibble. She fed me in much the same way. A hint of vanilla and almond hit my tongue first. I closed my eyes and groaned.

"You picked the best things, sweetheart." Our eyes met the minute mine popped back open and the smile on her face was everything. My heart skipped a whole fucking beat under the weight of that look.

"Thank you," she whispered to me.

I shook my head slightly and leaned in to kiss her lips that still had a tiny bit of frosting at the corner. "Told you I'd be respectful, but I never promised not to clean you up the fun way." As our mouths met, my tongue slipped out just enough to swipe away the tiny little hint of frosting that was left behind. "So fucking sweet, Court."

Her eyes sparkled with something I couldn't quite put my finger on as I pulled back from our brief kiss. "Flynn." The way she whispered my name sent a jolt of lust through me and suddenly there was nowhere else I wanted to be than the honeymoon suite with my new wife. Unfortunately for me, there was almost zero chance that my new, still very heartbroken wife would want to sleep with me, so I pulled back. We untangled our arms and turned to grin at the crowd as someone from the catering company began to pass out slices of cake to everyone.

"Is it bad that I wish they'd eat their cake and leave?" Courtney asked. I gently bumped into her side and grinned down at her.

"Honestly, I wished they all would disappear when we had our first dance."

"What are you two conspiring about over here?" I turned to see my younger sister, Mina. Her hair was down and straight around her shoulders. She wore a beautiful dress, but it was covered up by a shrug or shawl or whatever they were called. She looked like an old lady trying to cover up and keep warm.

"Mina, are you having fun?" Her shoulders bounced in answer before her eyes turned to my new wife.

"You got the better Robeson," she told Courtney. "I hope you realize that and treat my brother accordingly."

"I would never treat Flynn poorly."

"Not on purpose," Mina stated. I growled because it was my wedding day, and she didn't get to make my wife feel bad. Courtney placed her hand on my chest and smiled up at me.

"She's your sister. Let her say her peace."

"She's my little sister. It isn't her job to protect me from my wife."

Mina cocked her head to the side and took in the way Courtney and I stood united. Then she offered us both a genuine smile. "Never mind. I don't think anyone has reason to worry." She didn't wait around for a response. Instead, she turned on her heel and left. No one else seemed to notice as she all but fled our reception.

"She seems sad lately. Do you know what's bothering her?"

I shook my head. "No, but remind me once all this is over because I am going to start digging into it."

"Good. If you find out someone hurt her, I want in on the revenge."

My deep chuckle made my wife giggle up at me. "Sure thing, my little Nemesis."

"I'm not your enemy," Courtney scoffed.

"Nemesis, the Goddess of Vengeance, sweetheart."

"Oh, well, I won't complain if you want to compare me to a goddess." Her teasing tone made me smile. In truth, I worried about the wedding but dreaded the reception because I thought it would all be too much for Courtney to handle.

"You seem to be doing okay." It was a risky topic of discussion, but it felt wrong to ignore the elephant in the room if it was crushing her.

"I came to the same realization as your sister recently." Her quiet admission nearly floored me.

"You think you'll hurt me?"

"What?" she gasped and turned to face me. Her hand never left the spot where it rested in the center of my chest. "No!" That one word was a very vehement denial. "My realization was that you are the better Robeson man. If the roles were reversed, would you have sent me to marry Beckett?"

"Hell no!" I didn't even take the time to think over my response. "He's a fucking idiot for doing it."

"Exactly." Her slender fingers tapped my chest again and the diamonds from her wedding band caught the light and shined brightly. I took her hand in mine and examined the ring. Most married women wore two, their wedding and engagement band. Courtney's engagement band had come from Beckett. In a weird way, it made me happy to see that she had taken that one off and refused to put it back on.

"I can get you an engagement band to go with this," I said as my finger tapped the ring.

She shook her head. "To be honest, I hate the engagement ring Beckett got me. The setting sticks out too far and snagged on everything. I ruined two sweaters and scratched a couple of the kids by accident. Besides, Beckett always complained about how messy I got it. I'm an art teacher and an artist. There were always paint speckles and bits of clay that clung to it before I was able to clean it all up."

"We've already established that my cousin is an idiot. I'd be proud to see those paint speckles because it meant you didn't want to take it off even when you knew things might get messy." I hated that it was Beckett's ring we were talking about in that context, but I hoped that one day she might feel the same about mine.

Courtney didn't respond, but the way her eyes softened on me made me wonder what she was thinking. Unfortunately, mind reading wasn't one of my abilities.

"Are you two going to stand in the corner being secretive all night or join the party?"

I glanced up to see Courtney's parents standing there. Her mom's question had been a bit snippy, which I didn't understand.

"Mom?" Courtney questioned.

"You're being rude. Your guests…"

"Are here to celebrate our marriage. I think they'll understand that we needed a few moments to ourselves." My wife's shoulders stiffened with obvious tension. "What is your problem exactly?"

"It's nothing," her father answered instead. "Your mom is under a little stress."

"What kind of stress could you be under that you would come over here and insult my husband and me on our wedding day."

"It wasn't an insult," Courtney's dad tried to explain again.

"Her tone suggests otherwise, Dad."

My eyes bounced back and forth between Courtney and her parents as I tried to understand the new dynamic. I'd never seen them be anything but supportive of their daughter in the past. Then again, I supposed she was doing what they wanted before.

"It was so embarrassing to have Beckett show up and cause a scene. I think that if you two mingled more, people would forget about it."

I glanced around. No one seemed put off by the events during our wedding. "Everyone seems to be having a good time," I mentioned.

"That's what they want you to think. They're all talking about it." Courtney rolled her eyes at her mother's assessment, but I felt the way her body tightened even further with her mother's implications.

"Listen, Jill," I said in a warning tone. "We don't give two shits what anyone here thinks of Beckett's little performance earlier. That's a Beckett problem and doesn't reflect on us. If you think it does, then you are welcome to leave our party and go find Beckett, so the two of you can commiserate together. What you're not going to do is ruin our reception, or my wife's good mood, with your bullshit."

Courtney's father, Reed, grinned at me and then pulled

his wife into his side. "It's getting late for us older folks," he winked as if the words he spoke weren't the truth. "I wanted to congratulate you both, wish you the best moving forward, and…" He hesitated then but looked me in the eye with a stern expression plastered to his face where the jovial one had been moments ago. "I also came to warn you to be good to my baby girl, but I see that won't be an issue."

"No, sir. She's my priority now."

"Good. Keep it that way," Reed warned as he turned and pulled his wife away before she could say something to ruin the moment. Once they were gone, Courtney released a heavy sigh.

"Thank you for standing up to her. Normally, I would just brush it off or tell her to stop, but sometimes when I push back, she gets louder."

"Your mom has her priorities a little messed up."

"Trust me, she'll be riddled with guilt over it later. Sometimes, her emotions get the best of her and things don't always come out the way they should."

"Nemesis takes the back seat when Mom is involved. Good to know. I don't mind being the bad guy with your mother if she needs to be put in her place, sweetheart."

Courtney smiled and wrapped her arms around me. I pulled her in and tucked her close to offer her the comfort and warmth she needed. She felt so fucking good in my arms that I never wanted to let go. When my wife pulled back, I reluctantly let her slip from my arms.

"She was right about one thing, though. We do need to go mingle more and thank people for coming."

I scoffed out a half laugh at that. "They should be

thanking us. You know half these assholes only showed up in the hopes of seeing some drama."

"Oh my God! You are so right! My Aunt Peggy wouldn't have come otherwise. She didn't even RSVP to the wedding when it was supposed to be with Beckett. Her showing up is probably what really sent my mom into a tizzy. Her sister has always been a judgy beast."

"We should put on a show for her then. Make her wonder how you were ever engaged to another man just a couple weeks ago when we're obviously so madly in love with one another." I was teasing her, mostly because I knew she didn't feel that way about me, even if my feelings were a little more on the nose.

"Let's do this," Courtney announced as she held out her hand to me. "Do you know how to dirty dance, like in the movie?"

I laughed. "Fuck no, but I'll try anything to make everyone's tongues wag with jealousy and speculation."

"And you call me Nemesis!" she huffed out amidst her laughter.

I thanked my lucky fucking stars that I was able to marry a woman who had been a long-time friend. She was perfect. Once we were in the middle of the dance floor, I pulled her close, so one of her legs rested between mine and then I dipped her backward over my arm and swooped her in an arc until her bright, shining eyes caught back up to mine. I prayed to every god and goddess known to humankind right then and there that I would be able to keep her.

Chapter Eleven

COURTNEY

Flynn kept me so entertained on and off the dance floor for the rest of the night that I hardly remembered there was any drama surrounding my marriage to him. Thankfully, Beckett stayed clear of the reception, and no one else mentioned any of the drama. It made for a magical night, which was a surprise considering I'd been dreading it for two weeks.

As everyone else started to bow out of the party, I glanced across the room to see my new husband making his family laugh. He really was the best of them. I wondered again what might have happened if we had gotten together in high school. The knot of anxiety in my stomach made me realize, yet again, that there was no point in dwelling on a past that didn't happen. I also couldn't stop to think about my very uncertain future. I wasn't sure where Flynn saw this going between us, and I was too chicken-shit to have that conversation with him just yet.

I was also just tipsy enough to know that I wanted to sleep with my husband, and I hoped like hell that he would agree. It wasn't fair that my former fiancé had been slutting it up with every woman he could get his hands on and I had only ever been with him. I needed for that to change immediately. I quieted the other part of my brain, or maybe it was my lusty hormones, who insisted that wasn't the only reason I wanted to jump my husband's bones. It probably wasn't even the main reason. Flynn Robeson was a gorgeous man with a fit body, and his sense of humor only made him sexier. He threw his head back and laughed at something his father said, and a shiver of anticipation ran up my spine.

Bea said something to him and his head snapped around until our eyes met. He didn't even pause to excuse himself from the conversation with his family. My husband marched across the room in my direction with a radiant smile plastered to his handsome face. "Hey, where did you run off to?" he asked when he got close enough to be heard over the music that continued to pump through the speakers.

I hitched my thumb over my shoulder. "Bathroom. I thought it would be easier in this version of my dress, but trying to keep everything clean and avoiding wrinkles is a whole process."

"I bet. I could have helped you," he offered with a knowing smirk on his face.

"We're not at the 'sharing bathrooms' portion of our marriage yet, honey." He laughed at my teasing tone, but I was serious. We may have been friends since forever, but I was almost positive Flynn had never heard me so much as fart in public, let alone help me go pee in the bathroom.

"Fine, we'll work our way up to that." He winked at me as an unexpected yawn took me hostage. "Damn, boring my wife to death on our wedding night. I'll never live this down."

"It's been a crazy two weeks," I admitted as a tiny, nervous laugh erupted from me. The alcohol I'd consumed throughout the night probably didn't help. Still, the post-stress crash and alcohol warred with my overactive hormones who wanted to keep me awake long enough to fulfill their deepest desires. I hoped my husband would be onboard with the plan.

"We should call it a night," Flynn suggested. My agreement came in the form of a nod as I pushed in closer to his body and allowed him to shoulder some of my weight. "The question is, do we announce our departure or sneak out?"

"Sneak out. If we announce it, everyone will want to talk to us first, then it will be another hour of goodbyes, well-wishes, and fielding nosy questions."

"Sneaking out it is," Flynn agreed as he tugged me further back in the shadows. Once we were mostly out of sight of everyone, he grabbed my hand and pulled me along behind him as we all but ran for the exit of the ballroom. I yawned again as we made it to the elevator. "Good thing we have a room here. I don't think you'd make it back to my house without slipping into a coma."

I laughed at that as we rode the elevator up to the penthouse floor. "You're probably not wrong."

Was I supposed to bring up what I wanted now? Did we need to have some sort of adult conversation, or should I just wait to jump him once we got into our room?

The elevator dinged and opened to let us out. That ruled out a conversation before we entered our honeymoon suite. Nerves hit me as we got to the door. Flynn unlocked it and kicked it open with his foot. Just as I tried to walk inside, he reached an arm out to stop me, and had to kick the door open again. Before I could register what he was up to, my husband swooped in and scooped me up into his arms. He carried me into our room and kicked the door closed behind us.

"You didn't think I would ignore tradition, did you?" he asked as his eyes met mine. We were so damn close. His cologne, while subtle after wearing off over the course of the day, wrapped around my body and clung to me in the best way. I'd always loved the slightly spicy scent with a hint of the outdoors that he wore.

"Is that the only tradition we're keeping with?" I asked. Flynn allowed my body to slide down his as he set me back onto my feet and I didn't miss the fact that his body was interested, even if his brain wasn't all the way engaged.

"I'd understand if you didn't want to follow through with anything else," he admitted.

I shook my head. "No." His face fell, and he looked away. I realized he thought I meant that we wouldn't be sleeping together. I reached up and pulled his attention back to me. "I want to. I've only ever been with…" I fell short of saying another man's name when we were having the talk about whether to be intimate or not. "Can I be honest?"

"I'd prefer it, especially now."

"I don't want him to be the last person I was with. I also don't want you to think that is the only reason I want to do this."

"I'd understand if it was," he said, but I could hear the hint of hurt in his voice.

I shook my head again, denying that assumption. "No,

it's not. I know you've seen yourself in a mirror, Flynn." I cocked a brow up at him as I grinned and yanked on the lapel of his tux. "My husband is hot as fuck," I teased.

His mouth crashed down on mine in a searing kiss that left my knees weak, my heart hammering in my chest, and my mind completely blown. I didn't want Flynn to take control just yet, though. I was used to that with - the ex who I shouldn't be thinking of.

I unbuttoned and unzipped Flynn's pants and reached in to grab hold of him. My eyes widened in surprise at his girth because he was at least double the size of… Well, he was far larger than I was used to.

"What's that look?" he asked.

"Trying to figure out logistics."

"Logistics?" He was puzzled, but also slightly amused. That probably meant Flynn knew exactly what the problem was, and he wanted me to say it out loud. Instead, I shocked him when I dropped to my knees and licked the tip of his dick to catch the precum that had pooled there.

"Holy shit, Court," my new husband hissed as he grabbed hold of my hair and bunched it up into his fist. "You gonna suck my fat cock, sweetheart?"

I didn't answer. Once again, I shocked him as I reached up and yanked his pants down to his ankles along with his boxer briefs. I gripped his balls as my eyes shifted to look up at him. That hooded, sultry look would forever be stamped into my brain. If a look could make a woman's panties burn clean off her body, then my husband would be capable of doing just that. My pussy dripped for him as I leaned in and took his cock into my mouth. At first, I just teased him by slowly sucking on the head as I squeezed his balls and gave them a sharp tug.

"Son of a…" Flynn called out in a needy growl. "Take more of it," he demanded, and that time I relented and took his orders. My mouth stretched further than it ever had before, and while it was slightly uncomfortable, the noises my husband made were worth it. I slid one hand up his length as I sucked him down into my mouth as far as I could before my gag reflex kicked in.

"That's it, sweetheart. Breathe through your nose. You can take more. Let me see that pretty face dripping in tears as you choke on my dick."

Why in the hell was that so hot?

I did as he asked, and by the time he growled out his release as he shot warm jets of cum down my throat, I was desperate to have him inside me.

Chapter Twelve

COURTNEY

I woke up to the morning sun shining through the windows that neither of us thought to close the night before. I groaned at the audacity of the sun to shine so brightly when I wasn't ready for it yet. A gravelly chuckle made me turn my head to the side to see my husband lying there, obviously amused by my thoughts on the morning light. My eye drifted down of their own accord. My very naked husband took notice and quickly became excited at the prospect of going another round.

Honestly, I didn't even know a man could perform so many times in such a short window. We went three vigorous rounds the night before - four if you counted the oral orgasm he gave me when we waited on him to recharge that last time. I glance at the alarm clock on the nightstand. It had only been three hours since the last time and my husband, champion of all things sex apparently, had risen to the occasion once again.

I glanced back up to meet his eyes and realized he was even more amused than before. "I'll be honest with you. I've never had that much sex in a 24-hour period, and I'm not sure my body is ready for another." Truthfully, I was achy and sore. We hadn't exactly gone for the gentle love making most women dream about for their wedding nights.

Flynn sat up and threw the covers over his dick. "Ignore that."

"Kinda hard to do." I giggled as I said it and he cocked his head to the side and rolled his eyes at me.

"Did I hurt you last night?"

My head shook before I even registered his question. "No, not at all. Like I said, I'm not used to that much, or that vigorous, or…" My eyes drifted down to his lap, "Your size."

Flynn's answering grin spread from ear to ear and made his eyes twinkle with delight. "Is that so?"

I threw a pillow at his face. "You are such a man!"

"All man!" my husband added as he dove toward me and dug his fingers into my sides to tickle me. "All your man," he corrected. "We can draw a bath for you in the huge-ass tub in the bathroom. A soak might help."

"That sounds lovely, but maybe after I eat."

"How about you soak while we wait for room service to bring the food up, and I'll see if they can scrounge together some kind of over-the-counter pain killer too."

"You are setting the husband bar pretty high. You know you have to live up to this standard forever now, right?"

"I hope so," Flynn whispered against my ear before he placed a kiss at my temple and then hopped up to head to the bathroom. I am not ashamed to admit that I watched his ass until the damn wall got in the way. How did I not know the man had an award-winning ass?

Once I heard the water flowing steadily, I got up and grabbed Flynn's shirt off the floor and stuffed my arms through, then buttoned three of the buttons in the middle. When he noticed me, a smirk immediately bloomed across his handsome face.

"You do know I saw everything last night, right?"

"I know. That doesn't mean I don't feel weird walking around completely naked like my nudist husband."

His grin spread wider. "I like the sound of that."

"Being a nudist?"

"Being your husband."

I felt the heat in my cheeks and knew he could see what that did to me. The blush stole hot and fast across my face and up to the tips of my ears. I wondered if he truly meant that, or if he was just playing along and making the best of a weird situation.

"It's kind of strange to get used to being married," I admitted. "I feel like if I keep acknowledging the fact that you are my husband, it will sink in one day. Right now, it kind of feels like a dream."

"Good to know."

"What?" I questioned.

"Good to know I'm your dream husband. It makes being the real thing that much easier," he teased. "You might want to check the temperature on the water before it fills any further. I wasn't sure how hot you wanted it."

"Just shy of scalding my skin off is a good temperature."

"Damn woman," he hissed as I stuck my hand in. Not that I needed to, since I saw steam rising out of the tub. "You adjust and hop in. I'll go order room service. Any special requests?"

"French Toast."

"That's it?"

"Whatever else you order can be a surprise, but I really hope they have French Toast."

"Okay, beautiful. I'll be right back."

I took his shirt off and climbed into the tub gingerly as the heat stung my skin. I turned the hot water down a bit and swirled it around the tub before I sat all the way down and leaned back.

I was a little disappointed when Flynn didn't return to join me in the tub. For some reason, when he said he would run a bath for me to soak, my mind instantly envisioned us in there together with me snuggling into his body as he sat behind me. It was possible I had read one too many romance books over the years. Maybe that wasn't something men did.

"Hey," he called out after I'd been soaking long enough for the water to become tepid.

"Hey," I whispered back.

"Food is here. You looked so relaxed I didn't want to disturb you earlier."

"You came in here?"

His chuckle made me want to leap out of the tub and jump his bones. "Yeah, I debated on whether I should risk you hating me for disturbing you or if I should just leave you alone. When you didn't even notice I was back, I figured leaving you alone was the best option."

Well, shit. I guess I ruined my own fantasy by dozing off.

"You could have joined me," I told him as I ducked down further into the water to pull the plug.

"I'll keep that in mind for next time." He came over

with a warm towel in his hand and wrapped me up in it. "There's a robe on the back of the door."

Flynn left and as soon as I got the robe on, I followed him into the suite only to realize there was no one there. I looked around in confusion until I heard the sliding glass door open up.

"Sorry, I should have mentioned I brought everything out here. I thought you might enjoy a little sunshine with breakfast."

Breakfast on the balcony with my new husband. Yes, please.

As we both tucked into our food, I wondered how much a person would have to pay to live like this forever. It was a shame I was only a teacher, because I'd all but forgotten what it was like to live in my parents' home growing up, where there was a maid and cook who would prepare all our meals. Even though I lived in their pool house, I was responsible for cooking and cleaning for myself. As my mom once told me, "I don't pay for them to take care of you too. If you want that luxury, you'll have to marry well or change careers."

That was her version of a pep talk to keep me on track one of the times I thought about calling it quits with Beckett. I had to shake that thought off because if there were two people in the world who could ruin my first day with my husband, my ex-fiancé and mom fit the bill.

"How much longer do we have this suite?" I asked. When I planned the wedding and my honeymoon originally, I had chosen a smaller, cheaper room and only for an overnight, since Beckett and I were supposed to fly out the next day to an all-inclusive Caribbean resort. It wasn't the resort I hoped to stay at, but I hadn't been able to get Beckett to kick in any more money toward the honeymoon, so I had to go with one of the more budget friendly options and we couldn't even get the honeymoon suites let alone one of the over-the-water bungalows I really wanted to stay in.

"One more night and then we go home."

"Home," I parroted. "Crap, we never discussed what our living arrangements would look like."

"Well, we're married, and of the two of us, I'm the only one with my own home. I never said anything because I figured you would move in with me."

"Oh." I stared out at the puffy white clouds floating across a vibrant blue sky and then turned to my new husband. "Are you sure you want me to move in with you?"

"Court, we're married. Typically, a husband and wife live together. If you don't want to…"

"No, it's not that. I wouldn't feel right invading your space if you didn't want me there."

"Why in the hell would I not want you there?" The concern in his eyes was genuine and it was yet another reminder that Beckett had been the worst kind of fiancé and boyfriend before that. As if he plucked the thoughts straight from my mind, Flynn sighed and then leaned closer to take my hand in his. "Courtney, I know it's going to be an adjustment, but I am not Beckett. I don't know what the fuck he was thinking by not moving you in with him the minute you turned 18, or at the very least, as soon as you graduated from college. No matter how everything plays out, or whatever you decide down the road, so long as we are married and committed to that, I want you living in my house with me."

"Okay."

"I mean it," he said as he reached over and lifted my chin so that I couldn't hide from his relentless gaze. "If there's ever a question in your mind as to my intentions, you can come to me."

"I will." When he offered up a dubious look that said he didn't quite believe me, I tacked on, "I promise."

"Let's give this a couple months, and if you haven't run away yet, we'll plan a honeymoon. I'm sorry I couldn't get the time off right away, but with the short notice, it was too difficult to have everything covered."

"No, I get it. Besides, Beckett claimed the honeymoon I planned for us and took the tickets."

"Wait, didn't you guys split the cost of that?" Flynn asked. I felt my cheeks heat. There was no way I could tell him that I paid for the majority of it while Beckett only added about a third of the cost.

"That bastard didn't even chip in, and he took the tickets?"

"He paid some of it," I hedged.

"Come on, Court. I know my cousin. He's always looking for the best way to get someone else to foot the bill."

"I paid two-thirds of it," I admitted.

"Where were you going to go?"

"St. Lucia, there's an all-inclusive resort there with over-the-water bungalows, and I've always wanted to stay in one."

"You paid the majority of the price for one of those bungalows?" he asked.

"No. We were going to have a normal room looking out over the garden area."

"Not even a beach view?"

I was embarrassed to answer. "I couldn't afford the higher price for the view, so I figured it would all work out, since I didn't plan to stay cooped up in the room much anyway."

"Oh, my little Nemesis, there is so much wrong with that statement. Don't worry, when we plan our getaway, I will pay for the bungalow over the water and we will get plenty of use out of it." He wiggled his eyebrows up and down and then leaned over and planted a kiss right on my open mouth. Then, my new husband licked at my lips. "You always have such sweet things on your lips. How do you expect me to stay away?"

"I don't." The words slipped out before I could even process what I said. The minute his smirking face pulled away from mine, it hit me. "Shit. I-"

Flynn held a finger up to my lips to shush me. "Nope. Don't even think of taking that back. I'm going to take that statement to my dreams whenever you aren't around, so I can imagine tasting sweet little treats from all over your body."

"Maybe we should," I hitched my thumb over my shoulder at the room and Flynn got up and grabbed my hand as he headed back inside. I followed just as quickly, and the minute the sliding door was shut behind us, my husband ripped my robe off my body and tossed me onto the bed, fully naked. He slipped out of his matching robe and joined me.

Chapter Thirteen

COURTNEY

THE LAST ART class before my lunch break headed out with their teacher and I started to pick up the mess they left behind. Normally, part of the class was the cleanup time to teach them to be responsible, but that didn't work out because we had so much fun, even I lost track of time.

"What put that big ass smile on your face?"

I turned to see Beckett in my doorway, and the smile immediately slipped away. The bastard had not only stolen my honeymoon out from under me, not paid me back for the money I put into it, but apparently, he charged the woman he took in my place half the cost, which was more than he paid in.

"Aren't you supposed to be in St. Lucia on the trip I paid for?" I asked, knowing there should have been three more days on the trip.

"Thanks to you, I had to come back early."

I laughed at that. "How in the hell did I cause that all the way from here?"

Beckett rolled his eyes. "You know exactly what you did.

Why couldn't you just leave it alone? You married another man; it's not like you can be angry that I took a woman on vacation."

"We started dating when we were teenagers. I'm 25 now. Even if you take away the time we were minors, you still had seven years to take me on a vacation or even a weekend getaway, and you never did."

"So, this is about us." His smug face itched to have my fist introduce itself.

"No, Beckett. It is not about us. I was blind to a lot of shit I should have never put up with, but believe me, I'm over it. People tagged me in that stupid post and I answered their question, end of story."

"You told them that you paid two-thirds of the honeymoon cost." The way he said it sounded like an accusation.

"Because I did!" I shouted at him before I realized we were still at school. "Look, you can't be here. This is my job. You never liked when I dropped into your office, and I don't appreciate you coming here and trying to upset me simply because…" It occurred to me that he still hadn't answered why he was back, beyond trying to point the finger at me. "Why in the hell are you back here and not in St. Lucia?"

"Brandy got pissed off after she found out how much you paid for the trip."

"Oh, yeah, considering you made her pay half of the total. I guess I can see why she'd be angry, since you managed to turn a profit by swindling us both into paying for it."

"I didn't swindle anyone!" he ground the words out through clenched teeth. "She trashed the room and we got kicked out. I managed to get my ticket changed. Not sure what Brandy did."

"You left her there by herself without a hotel to stay at?"

"She is the reason we got kicked out."

"Because you cheated her! God, Beckett! What happened to you?"

He growled something under his breath that I didn't catch.

"You know what? Never mind. I don't really care anymore."

"We need to talk about some things, Courtney."

"Like what? When are you going to pay me back for the vacation you stole?"

"I didn't steal it, and no. We need to talk about when you're coming back and…"

I laughed. "I am not coming back to you, Beckett. The sooner you understand that, the better off we will all be." I glanced at the clock. "You have killed half of my lunch break. I need you to leave."

"Please, meet me tonight for dinner. At the very least, we need to talk about swapping each other's stuff we left behind."

"Fine. Please leave, and text me where to meet you."

He tipped his head in some weird, Beckett-style acknowledgment, and then left without another word. Meanwhile, I sent a text to let my husband know his cousin had been here to see me and that he wasn't done with the conversation.

> Courtney: Beckett came to my school today.

Flynn: Did he pay you back for that trip?

Courtney: 😏 I wish. I told him I couldn't talk here, so he asked me to meet him for dinner tonight.

Flynn: Where and when?

Courtney: Don't know he's supposed to text me that info. Maybe if I'm lucky, he'll have my money.

Flynn: Don't hold your breath, sweetheart. Although, I can lend you a bat if you want to take out his kneecaps, Nemesis!"

Courtney: Don't tempt me. Gotta go get ready for my next class. See you tonight.

FOR THE FIRST time in my life, I hoped that Beckett stood me up. Not that our little dinner meeting was a date, but I really didn't want to see him twice in one day. Just my luck, he was there before I even showed up. I guess he didn't want to take any chances on missing me.

I ignored the hostess and walked to the table. When I stood there, Beckett got out of his seat. "Do we really need to do this?" I asked. Home, a good meal with Flynn, a shower, and bed were calling my name in equal measure.

"If you're serious about us being over then I guess we do."

I rolled my eyes and took my seat. "You don't even know how to take any of the blame for what happened, do you?"

"Look, I'll get you your half of the trip money." He huffed.

"Half?" I chuckled as if what he said was a joke.

"Fine, I'll get you back what you paid in."

"That would be great. Are we done now?"

"We haven't even ordered drinks yet, for Christ's sake."

It was only then that I took a look around and realized the place was dimly lit, there was a fake candle on the table, and wine glasses were ready. The waiter showed up before I had the chance to question Beckett on the atmosphere. He tried to order one of my favorite wines, but I shook my head and got the man's attention. "I don't want wine. What I need is a strong cup of coffee with cream."

"And you, Sir? Do you still want the wine?"

"No. I'll have water for now," Beckett waved his hand as if to rudely dismiss the waiter.

"Thank you," I called out to him as he walked away.

"What are you doing drinking coffee this late? That's not like you."

"I'm exhausted, Beckett. It's been a long day. This isn't the place I want to be and quite frankly, you're the last person I want to spend time with. Can we please get this over with?"

"Do you really not care about all the years we were together?"

"They're over. You saw to that."

He huffed and I moved to stand until his hand reached out and held my arm. "Please, I'm sorry. You're right. Let's get this over with." When I took my seat again, the waiter came over with Beckett's water and my coffee. I told him we needed a minute, just to get rid of him, though I didn't plan to stay long enough to order anything beyond my coffee.

"I already have your things in a box in the trunk of my car," he told me. He must have known deep down that I wouldn't agree to his last-ditch effort to keep me. Then again, he probably didn't really want that. I was a comfortable, stable part of his life. Truthfully, I wondered if I amounted to much more than furnishing in his life before. My presence was only ever tolerated when it was convenient to Beckett.

How did I not see that I was never his priority?

As the thought rolled around in my mind, Beckett reached across the table and grabbed hold of my hand. "Courtney, I know you're mad right now. I know I fucked up, and that things seem like they're unfixable. I need you to remember all the years we were together. All the good times we had meant something to both of us. I need you to promise me something."

"What?"

"Promise me you won't sleep with my cousin."

"We're married and you've slept with at least three women that I know of since we split, and I don't think it would be a far leap to guess there were more."

"It's different with Flynn and you know it."

"You told me to marry him, remember?"

"Yeah, as a convenience, not a real marriage."

"Oh, so it's okay if you sleep with other people, but I'm supposed to live by a different set of rules? You are something else!"

"It's not like that. It's just... He's family. You have to

understand how complicated that would be when... If we get back together in the future."

I wanted to laugh and cry at the same time. I couldn't believe the audacity to try to keep me from sleeping with someone else. There was no doubt he would say the same things even if Flynn wasn't his cousin. He would always have an excuse for why he should be able to do something and I should just sit patiently in the corner and twiddle my thumbs until he got his fill of other people.

When I didn't agree or say anything at all, Beckett squeezed my hand to get my attention back on him. "You haven't slept with him already, have you?"

I didn't bother to answer him. Instead, I stood up and grabbed my purse. "You can leave my box of things with my parents. I don't want to see you again. I'll drop anything of yours off with your parents."

"Please, don't do this."

I turned to leave and could have sworn I saw Flynn walk out of the restaurant. I got ready to chase after him, but Beckett caught hold of my arm again. "You never answered the question."

"And I don't plan on it because what I do and who I do or don't do it with is none of your damn business Beckett Robeson." He flinched back as I snatched my arm out of his grip.

Chapter Fourteen

FLYNN

COURTNEY DIDN'T ANSWER HIM.

I rubbed my hand over my chest as it really settled in that she refused to tell him that we had not only slept together on our wedding night but continued to do so. We hadn't missed a single night, or morning for that matter, of getting very acquainted with one another's bodies. Beckett didn't need those details, but she could have at least said it was already too late to demand her fidelity, especially from me - her husband.

She didn't. I had planned on putting my cousin in his place and telling him to stay the fuck away from my wife, but when she refused to answer, I had to wonder if it was because she was holding out hope that they would still get back together. I had missed the beginning of their conversation because my last meeting of the day ran well over when it was supposed to end.

I hated that I wasn't there to walk her in and put up a united front against Beckett, but considering what I'd just witnessed, maybe it was for the best that time got away from me at work. How else would I know that she still wasn't over him. I wasn't stupid. They had been together most of their lives as friends, dating, and as an engaged couple. It took time to get over a relationship that long. He was her first love, and that wasn't something I would ever even think possible. Still, when she didn't tell him we had already been intimate, something inside me broke. Maybe it was my hope for our future.

We hadn't talked about taking our marriage to a real place, so that was my fault. I assumed when we had sex, and then kept having it, that it was a mutual decision to behave as a truly married couple moving forward. I hoped that it worked out for us in the end. Courtney never said if she was on the same page with me. I was beginning to think her silences spoke louder than anything she did say.

By the time she got home, I pretended to be crashed out on the couch in the living room. My wife tried to wake me up to come to bed, but I groaned and flipped over so my back was to her.

"I know you're not asleep. I saw you at the restaurant just before I left," she said in her normal speaking voice. She waited to see if I would turn back over, and when I didn't, she turned and walked away. I was up and out of my house before she had to get up and get ready for work. Maybe it was immature, but I wasn't ready to face her. Part of me didn't want to know the reason she refused to answer him, or what kind of agreement they came to after I walked away.

IT WAS NEARLY lunchtime when my assistant, Jeff, let me know that I had an unscheduled visitor. There was no reason it should have been Courtney, though that was why I told him to send them in. I wondered if maybe she hated sleeping alone the night before as much as I did. I was not pleasantly surprised when my door opened and my cousin walked in, only to turn and shut the door behind him.

"We need to talk."

"I don't see why," I answered back before shifting my attention back to the file in front of me. None of the information there made it to my brain because I was too busy trying to talk myself out of throwing my cousin out the window and down into the middle of mid-day traffic.

"Flynn, she's still in love with me." He tossed out a laugh that sounded more nervous than self-assured. "She'll always love me. I was her first everything."

"How quickly you forget. You were also her first heartbreak and her second and third, and..." I stopped and pretended to think about it for a minute. "How many times did you break her over the years?"

"I didn't break Courtney. We've had some disagreements, but none of it enough to stop me from holding that number one spot in her heart."

"Is that why you let her go, so you could fuck around on her, and you didn't think she would care if you were on a break?" I asked. He started to nod and then caught himself.

"I was doing you a favor. How the hell else were you going to find a wife in time?"

It was my turn to laugh. "I could have found a wife a year ago when the money became available to me at 25, Beckett. It wasn't that important to me."

"But Sean's company." My cousin's brows furrowed inward as he mentioned the reason I ever even considered getting married in the first place - to save my father's dying business.

"My dad's business isn't really my problem, Beckett. I'd love to help him out, but he wouldn't have held it against me if I chose not to marry until I found the girl of my dreams."

"Then you can get an annulment."

I shook my head. "Nope. Not gonna do that. First of all, I'm married now and have to stay married for at least six months in order to fulfill the conditions of the Will. Then there's the other pesky little problem."

"What problem?"

I stood and walked over to the window to look down at all the people marching around on the street. "Remember, when you see her happy with someone else, whether it is me or another man eventually, you were the one who pushed her there. You cheered as she went, all so you could fuck other women without feeling guilty for it." I chuckled at his puzzled image reflected in the window. "Must be nice to be able to do your random women without having to hide. Then again, I think sneaking around felt more appealing to you, didn't it?"

"I don't know what you're talking about."

"I might not have proof, but I'm also not stupid. Courtney thinks were each other's one and only but people talk. You fucked around on her in high school and did the same while you were in college. You've probably already fucked your way through all the women at your office too."

"Okay, Mr. High and Mighty, why didn't you ever tell her?""

"Because I didn't have any proof and never thought she'd believe me without it."

"You always wanted her, but she chose me, asshole." The fantasies of shoving my cousin out the window started to feel like the only option the more he ran his mouth. He never denied that he cheated on her. If I were in his shoes and someone accused me, and I hadn't done it, I would scream it from the rooftops.

"Well, she's married to me." I shrugged and offered him a smug look as I turned around to face him again.

"She'll never sleep with you," Beckett argued.

"We had an amazing wedding night together and are married in every legal sense of the word - including that part about consummation."

"You're a fucking liar!"

"Am I?"

Someone gasped and I turned to see Courtney there in the doorway. It was her back, because she had already started to run from my office. *Fuck!*

Before I could get my ass in gear, Beckett chased after her. I wondered if she would kill him or take him back. I wasn't sure if she heard the part about me accusing him of cheating or if she'd just walked up when I mentioned that we had already consummated our marriage. Either way, my anger over her not telling him about us fucking was dwarfed by what she must think of me.

Chapter Fifteen

COURTNEY

I MANAGED to slip out of my husband's office without either of them catching up to me. I know Beckett gave chase, because I heard him before the elevator doors closed. Whether Flynn came after me or not was a mystery. I couldn't believe he taunted his cousin with our sex life, like it was some soap opera and only existed to provide drama to weaponize against people.

And he calls me Nemesis.

I scoffed at the thought of my recent nickname. Then, I pulled my phone out and sent a text to my best friend.

> Courtney: I need you. Are you home today?

> Hadley: I'm here and yay for three-day weekends that start on a Friday.

> Courtney: Be there soon.

It took longer than I wanted it to, but eventually I managed to get to Hadley's apartment.

"Hey bitch! Get in here." She yanked me inside her place and locked the door behind us. "Which one of the men in your life put that sour look on your face?"

"Both of them."

"Both?" she asked as she took a glass down and poured a healthy amount of wine.

"What is that?" I asked, not recognizing the bottle.

"This is the finest Moscato less than $10 can buy." Hadley chuckled as my lips turned down and I scrunched my nose.

"Why?"

"Not all of us can afford to be wine snobs, babe."

"Not all of us can afford to drink shitty wine, friend," I called back. It had been a bitch of a day though, so I took the glass from her and didn't bother to do anything other than gulp that shit down in a way that probably made all the other wine snobs in the world cry out for the injustice of it all.

"That tastes like the time you made me drink Boone's Farm straight from the bottle when we were in high school."

"In my defense, you refused to steal wine from your house," Hadley reminded me.

"Because my parents would have noticed even if a fifty-dollar bottle went missing, never mind the more expensive stuff."

Hadley shrugged. "Well, that's why we had to resort to having Edwin Milton buy a couple bottles."

"Oh my God! You got that shit off a legitimate crackhead?"

Hadley giggled. "It's not like he opened it and dumped a rock in there or something."

"I feel like I need to brush my tongue all these years later."

"Aw, stop making fun of poor Milton. He was good to us."

"To you, maybe."

"Feeling calmer now?" Hadley asked as I plopped down onto her sofa. My best friend had always been a master at distraction techniques.

"Thanks," I muttered.

"Now, tell me what happened." I watched as she pulled her midnight black hair up into a big fluffy ball on top of her head. To call it a messy bun would have been a disservice to all the artfully cute and messy hairdos out there. My best friend didn't care if it looked good. She just wanted all of it out of her face for a bit. I chuckled as the elastic band she used to secure it popped.

"Damn it!" she huffed. "I think that was my last one."

"Sorry about your thick hair problems. I'll buy you a new pack later."

"Fine. Tell me about your boy troubles." She seemed to think about that for a minute. "Is it weird that all your boy troubles stem from one family?"

"Hadley!" I whined.

"Okay, okay, tell me all about it. What happened today?"

"Well, the thing is, I have to back up and tell you what happened yesterday, first."

"Oh shit, why didn't you call yesterday."

"I did. You didn't answer." Hadley glared down at her phone as if it personally offended her.

"I don't see any missed calls."

"It doesn't matter." I sighed and then told her everything that happened, starting with the disaster of a dinner meetup and all the way until I ran from my husband's office straight to my best friend's house.

"Wow. That's…" she sighed and then turned to face me. "Can I be honest?"

"I didn't come here to get you to tell me how I look in a new pair of jeans. I came to you with boy trouble. That requires honesty."

"Fair." Hadley took a deep breath and then let it out slowly before she spoke. "I suspected Beckett of screwing around on you before too."

"What? Why didn't you tell me?"

"Same reason as Flynn. I didn't think you would take it too well if I didn't bring you proof. All I had was a feeling and the weird way he didn't want you to move in with him once you both graduated. It never made sense to me."

"Hindsight is a bitch, because looking back, there are a lot of things I overlooked."

"Yeah, well, I'm still a shitty friend for not pointing them out, but Beckett's been in your life longer and I didn't want to lose you if I was wrong."

"I understand. What made you think he was cheating, though?"

"I overheard some women talking about being with him, but everyone knows we're friends. I had no way of knowing if they were just trying to plant a seed to break you up or if it was the truth."

"You believed them, though?"

"Yes, I did. Beckett has always given off a slimy vibe.

He's charismatic, so most people ignore that and focus on his charm. He never charmed me."

"Yeah, you have always hated him."

"I don't hate him. I just didn't like him for you and didn't trust him as far as I could throw him. I'd have to care about the asshole to hate him."

"What am I going to do?" I asked her after we both sat there quietly for far too long.

"About Beckett? You already married another man. I say ghost his ass and forget he ever existed in your life."

"Obviously," I rolled my eyes as I said that and then smiled at my friend. "I meant about the mess with Flynn. It feels like no matter what I do, everything is going to come out wrong. I know he was mad at me, and I think it was because when Beckett asked me not to sleep with Flynn, I didn't tell him that it was too late."

"I'm sure that did hurt Flynn. It probably felt like you were ashamed to have gone there with him."

"I'm not. I wasn't. That's so wrong."

"Maybe so, but I guarantee that's how he felt."

"How do you know?"

"Because that's how I would have felt if I were in his shoes."

"Dammit, how do I fix this? I'm angry that he was so cavalier about our intimate moments. They're supposed to be private between the two of us only."

Hadley took her time before she answered me. "What you have is a little communication problem. I'd bet a lot of money that Flynn doesn't know that you *never* talk about your sex life."

"I kind of did with him after our first night."

"Well, that's new. I guess that makes it harder for him to understand why you didn't tell Beckett."

"Yeah, I suppose it does. I'll talk to him, but for now, can I spend the night with you? I don't want to deal with the adult relationship stuff right now."

"You are always welcome here, but only for one night, because any more than that is wallowing and wallowing leads to festering, and then things start to deteriorate further."

"I get the picture. I promise, one night only, then I'll go home and talk to Flynn." I turned my phone off and lounged back on Hadley's couch as she moved closer to me and hugged into my side.

"It's going to be okay, bestie. You just need a night to clear your head and gain some perspective."

Chapter Sixteen

FLYNN

I JOLTED awake and before my brain came online to tell me why, my heart started to race. I was on the couch, in my living room, and all the lights were on. That wasn't normal. A quick glance at the clock in the kitchen told me I'd dozed off for only an hour. Courtney didn't have work because of the three-day weekend, so after the disaster in my office with Beckett, I came back home to try to catch up to her here.

How in the hell had I fallen asleep on the couch?

It dawned on me in the next second that the house was too quiet.

"Courtney!"

I jumped up and ran to our bedroom only to find the bed still made and nothing had changed from how it was left the day before. Where the hell could she be? I went back to the living room and found my cell phone burrowed down into the cushions. Once I dug it out, it was clear that my wife hadn't tried to call or message me either. It had already been four hours since she left my office.

I tried to call her, but it immediately kicked to voicemail.

Either she had her phone off or my wife decided to block me.

Great!

I sent a text to her next.

> Flynn: Sweetheart, I need you to call or message me that you're okay. You can hate me if you need to, but please let me know you're not hurt or in trouble somewhere.

I wanted to add that she needed to let me know she hadn't gone to my cousin, but that seemed like the wrong thing to do. I was pretty sure she hated him more than me.

When another hour passed, I got up and left. "Where would she go?" I asked myself on the way to the car. The fucked up thing is that I didn't know. There were things I still hadn't learned about my wife. Despite the fact that we had been friends since before high school, there was a certain distance I maintained from Courtney over the years to spare myself the heartache of having to see her happy with someone else, especially since that someone else was my assholish cousin.

There were two people who might know more than me, though I really didn't want to go there and admit I was failing their daughter. Still, she might go there, back to the pool house where she lived before we got married. Once I thought about the fact that she used to live there, it dawned on me that my wife had not brought a lot of her things to the house we shared. It was as if she had been waiting for the other shoe to drop and didn't want to get too comfortable.

I scoffed at myself for not seeing it sooner. She wasn't all in and I was too complacent to see it. The drive over to the Parker family's house turned into a steady stream of what-if scenarios. I wasn't normally a person who dwelled in that space because self-doubt was a killer of dreams, but she was more important than anything else I had ever done in my life. My business could go to hell, friendships, even my family could be pushed aside while I accomplished my goals, but Courtney... I needed her in a way that made everything else fall to the wayside.

I didn't even get a chance to knock on the door before it opened and I stood there facing Reed Parker, Courtney's dad.

"Hey," he called out to me as he glanced around my shoulder as if looking for something - or someone. "Where's Courtney?"

"That's what I was here to find out." The panic that gnawed at my stomach hit a little harder.

"She's not here, and I don't think she pulled up at the pool house without me knowing either." He stepped back and left room for me to enter. "Why don't you fill me in on why you have no clue where your wife is while we walk out to the back to see if she's there?"

I nodded my head and explained everything that had gone down the past two days concerning his daughter, Beckett, and me. Reed never said a word as he took it all in and we walked through his stately house to the sliding glass door that led out to the deck that overlooked the pool below and the pool house that was clearly dark and without a car parked in the drive leading up to it.

"We've come this far, might as well go the whole way." I followed Reed down the stairs and out onto the lawn, all the while we both remained silent. Once we got to the pool house, Reed entered a code on the door and headed inside. His face slipped into a frown as he took in the space his daughter occupied prior to our marriage. "She didn't take a whole lot with her, did she?"

I shook my head as I looked around at all the little things that made the space uniquely hers, like her easel and paints. The paintings, many of which had her signature on them. "Jesus," I whispered as I took the space in.

"Obviously, my daughter hasn't settled into married life yet. How is it that she's been living with you since your wedding and all of her stuff is still here?"

"I don't know. I thought…" I spun in a slow circle and took it all in again. "I thought we were going to give it a real shot, but…" I had no words for the fact that I was a blind moron who hadn't realized that his wife was having nothing more than an extended sleepover with him and hadn't actually moved in.

Reed's hand clapped down on my shoulder and he squeezed. "If there's one thing married life has taught me, it is that men are generally the blind ones in the relationship. The women see everything, and they aren't afraid to hold it against you that you don't." He sighed and then tipped his head toward the couch that looked out a sliding glass door toward the pool. I nodded my agreement and we sat.

"I don't know how to fix everything. Did I doom us by agreeing to the marriage even when I knew that it wasn't what she wanted?"

Reed chuckled. "Son, I hate to tell you, but if a part of my daughter didn't want to marry you, she wouldn't have even entertained doing it."

My eyes tracked over to Reed's amused face. He had the same russet hair color as his daughter, with exception of a little gray that had started to sneak in around his temples. Courtney looked more like her mother but inherited her coloring from her father. That was probably for the best as Jill was always a little washed out and pale, especially when combined with her naturally light blonde hair. His blue-gray eyes stared straight at me and almost dared me to contradict him.

"I call her Nemesis."

"I wasn't aware that you two were in competition for anything."

"We're not." I chuckled at the memory of how she earned that nickname. "I call her that after the Greek Goddess of Vengeance."

Reed burst out laughing and slapped me on my knee. "Shit, Flynn," he managed to choke out between the laughter that died off to a chuckle. "Maybe you see more of her than I gave you credit for. You think she only agreed to marry you as some sort of payback for Beckett offering her up to you."

"I think that was a big part of it. She did it to hide from him and her heartbreak just as much, though."

Reed shook his head. "No, I don't think my daughter has been in love with him for a long while now. She thought she was because they'd invested so much time in trying to stay true to some dream they cooked up as children. The truth was, that boy didn't make my daughter happy. She was content and comfortable enough to go with the flow, but that was it. Beckett is a selfish prick who never deserved my daughter."

I nodded because what else could I say?

"He comes by that shit honestly. No offense, I know Marty is your uncle, but that fucker is just as bad - worse even."

That was news to me. The Parkers had always been exceptionally tight with my aunt and uncle. It was how Courtney and Beckett grew so close as children to begin with. "I thought all of you were friends?"

"We were. Don't get me wrong, sometimes you have friends - even good ones - who you know aren't the best people. Gayle is as solid as they come, but Marty has always been the friend who I took at face value and didn't look too closely, for fear of what I might learn that would put me in a compromising situation."

"If you thought that poorly of him, why would you trust your daughter to his son?"

"We're not our parents, Flynn. I thought I was doing the right thing, and that she would outgrow him. Courtney did just that, but the problem was that she didn't realize she had outgrown him because my little girl was still hung up on that silly dream about the future they planned when they were too young to understand what it all meant."

We sat there in silence for a few minutes, taking in everything. I was about to get up and leave when Reed heaved out a heavy sigh.

"Not a fan of you discussing my daughter's sex life with Beckett, or me for that matter. I get why you had to tell me what was said, but I'd prefer to think of my baby girl as a virgin who could still go cloister herself away in a convent somewhere, never to be touched by a man." The sharp look he gave me was almost enough to pierce skin.

"As a man, not thinking about the woman in question as my daughter, I get it. It's obvious you care about Courtney. If I were a man in love with a woman, and I had to face down her ex who wanted to keep stringing her along while he had his fun, I'd probably have thrown it in his face too."

"I already know it was the wrong move. It didn't hit me why she never answered him until she got angry with me for doing it. I thought maybe it was because she wanted to keep her options open where he was concerned."

"We men are fools," Reed put in.

"Yeah, it took me a minute, but I got it. She didn't owe him that truth and she didn't want to share it with him. My Nemesis was playing the long game, in a way. It hurt him more to stew on the unknown than it did to face the truth of what was happening between Court and me."

"I'm sure that was a little of it, but I think mostly it boils down to my daughter being a private person. Pretty sure she doesn't even tell Hadley about her sex life, and that girl is all about oversharing."

"Hadley," I whispered, and then wanted to kick myself for not thinking of her sooner. I turned to look at my father-in-law with narrowed, accusatory eyes then. His response was to laugh in the face of my suspicion.

"Yep, figured you'd think of her eventually, but I didn't want to bring up the possibility of my girl being at her best friend's place until you were able to talk through some things first. Can't have you going after her all half-cocked and getting it wrong." He winked at me to let me know he was sort of teasing. "I like you for my daughter. There was a time when I confided in my wife that I wished you were the one Courtney was hung up on." He shook his head as if that conversation did not go well.

"Jill didn't agree?"

"No, she was hung up on the wrong Robeson for some fucked up reason too. Wasn't until recently that I realized why, but when I did, it made it all so much worse."

"What do you mean?" I had a sinking suspicion I knew where he was going but hoped like hell I was wrong.

"I wanted to put a private investigator on Beckett, because I had a suspicion he was stepping out on my girl, but my wife wouldn't let me."

"That's weird, isn't it?" I asked.

Reed nodded and looked sick about whatever he was going to reveal to me. "I think she was afraid the PI might focus on her as well. I've suspected she's having an affair for a while now, too. I was more concerned for my daughter than finding out the truth for myself, though. It was the other reason I wasn't sure about Beckett being in her life in a romantic way. I thought maybe I was projecting my own relationship issues onto my daughter's."

"You don't think they were getting together, do you?" I asked, feeling sick. Courtney would not recover from her mother fucking someone she had been engaged to.

"No, but I think maybe it is someone close to him. She all but panicked when I brought up the idea of using a PI."

"My uncle," I guessed.

"That's my guess. We've always been close friends, but in recent years Jill and Marty have been closer." He cleared his throat and looked away. "I should have said or done some-thing sooner, but I didn't want to taint my daughter's relationship with everything. Little did I know that prick was all too happy to rid himself of my girl."

"A move I think he regrets now."

"Only because he thinks he will lose her forever," Reed said. "He has always been a weak spot for my daughter. His problem is that he assumed he always would be. He also doesn't know how to work for anything worth having, and that includes a relationship with my daughter."

My father-in-law stood and looked around the room before he spoke again. "You should take a couple of these with you, so when you bring my daughter home, there's no question that your future is together."

I nodded and glanced around. "Any clue which are her favorites?"

He chuckled. "If they're hanging on the wall, stands to reason, they're her favorites."

"That narrows it down," I muttered sarcastically. My wife had so many canvases on the wall that you wouldn't know the walls were white underneath it, unless you took a peek behind something.

"Anything worth having is worth working for," Reed reminded me. "Especially when it involves my baby girl."

"I'll take a few of the smaller ones, but I want her to pack the rest up herself. I'll do more harm than good if they end up damaged because I didn't protect them properly while moving them."

"There it is. The reason I always liked you better." Reed laughed as he walked toward the door. "You use your brain sometimes."

AN HOUR LATER, I pulled up to the apartment building where Hadley lived and made my way inside. She didn't live in a place with a fancy doorman. My wife's best friend was a teacher without the family money to fall back on. I was able to walk right up to her third-floor apartment and knock on the door without anyone stopping me.

When the door cracked open ever so slightly, Hadley peeked up at me from the little space available. "What do you want, Flynn?"

"My wife," I demanded.

"What if she doesn't want you?"

"Then I would like to hear that from her. If she doesn't want to talk to me right now, needs some space, or whatever then I will respect her wishes, but I need to hear it from her. I need to see that she's okay."

Hadley sighed as a piece of her black hair fell into her eyes from a blob of hair on top of her head big enough that it could have been used to smuggle a small child. She rolled her bright green eyes at me and then closed the door to remove the chain latch before she pulled it wider to let me in.

The first thing I saw - the only thing - was my wife staring out the window like the answers to all her problems were just out of reach. When she finally turned toward me, I couldn't hold myself back. I crossed the room and pulled her into my arms. "I'm sorry. I should have never shared our personal business with him," I admitted.

"And you call me Nemesis," she whispered into my chest. If she could make a joke, then we would be okay. We just needed to get on the same page with everything first.

Chapter Seventeen

COURTNEY

"Would you please come home, so we can talk things out?"

My eyes lifted to see Hadley across the room. She gave me a slight nod of her head before she walked off to her bedroom to give us some privacy. "What you did was not okay."

"I know."

"I won't allow another Robeson man to walk all over me."

"I know."

I shook my head as a queasy feeling in my stomach made me reevaluate my last statement. "I'm sorry, that wasn't a fair thing to say to you."

"No," Flynn said as he gently moved me back so that he held me at arm's length. "You're entitled to feel however you want, Court. It's been a whirlwind to say the least. One minute you were engaged to my cousin and the next you were married to me. You didn't even get a decent amount of time to grieve the loss of one relationship before you were thrown in the next one. When we started this together, it was an arrangement. We blurred those lines from the beginning, but I think maybe that's part of our problem."

"You regret the things we've shared?" I asked him as that sinking feeling in the pit of my stomach grew into a giant void that threatened to swallow me up at any moment. Flynn sighed and shook his head vehemently.

"No, not at all. My only regret is not giving you time to adjust first. I want you, sweetheart. There's no doubt about that, but I want you the right way. I don't want you to be confused or to resent me in the end for trampling all over you and pushing too hard for something you're not ready for."

"I'm pretty sure it was me who pushed for our wedding night," I teased to try to alleviate the thick tension that threatened to form a wall between us. Flynn's face remained serious as he pulled me in for another hug.

"Do you want to stay here for the night with Hadley, or…" He let the sentence dangle there with the hint of an invitation to come back home with him. It was still weird for me to think of his place as *home*. I lived there, but everything was his from before I was in the picture. Maybe Flynn was right, and we had both jumped in feet first without really taking the time we needed to sort ourselves, let alone what we were to each other.

"I want to come back. Hadley should get to enjoy what's left of her long weekend without having to mop up my tears or babysit my crazy emotions."

"I don't mind," my bestie called out, letting me know that we truly had no privacy in her tiny apartment.

"I'll meet you back at the house."

"You don't want to ride with me?" Flynn seemed almost hurt by me wanting to get there on my own.

"I would, if it weren't for the fact that my car is parked downstairs too, and I don't really want to have to worry about coming back for it later."

"Yeah, sorry, I forgot." Flynn backed up and then took another step backward toward the door. "I'll see you at home?"

"I'm right behind you, I promise." He offered a small smile and then left me there in my best friend's apartment. Once he was gone, Hadley came back out of her bedroom.

"Well?"

"I don't know," I shrugged.

"He apologized, right?"

"Yeah, but where do we go from here? He's right. We jumped right into this. I jumped right into this," I corrected. "I was running from what Beckett did and buried all my anger and sadness. The wedding, our night together, the days after…" I sighed. "It was all a distraction."

"Except you're missing the most important part of the equation," my friend informed me.

"What's that?"

"You were happy being distracted by Flynn and you weren't all that sad about losing Beckett."

THE FIRST THING I noticed when I got back to Flynn's house was that a couple of my smaller paintings were sitting propped against the wall. "What are they doing here?" I asked.

"I realized today that you never really moved in."

"Of course I did."

"No, you didn't. The only thing you have here are some of your clothes and the shit you use in the bathroom. There's no nicknacks, paintings, or all the other little touches that come with a person making a space theirs."

"Well, it's not my space."

"See, that's the thing, it is. We got married. You were supposed to move in here with me. You've just been sleeping over, though."

"I see." It felt like Flynn punched me in the chest with those words. He wasn't wrong. I hadn't moved in, but I also didn't want to rock the very precarious boat we had been floating around in since the wedding.

"How do we do this?" I finally asked.

My husband shrugged his shoulders. "One step at a time."

"That sounds oddly simple."

"I want to give you some space to figure things out, Court. I want you here with me, but you need to want it too." Before I could interject anything, he threw his hands up in the air to stop me. "You need to take the time to really work through the Beckett situation."

"It won't matter. I'll never go back to him."

"That might be the case, but it doesn't mean you would have chosen to be with me under normal circumstances."

I couldn't argue with that. Flynn was right. "Okay, but what does that mean for our current living situation?"

"You can have the master bedroom. I'm going to sleep on the couch until I get a bed in the spare room." One of his spare rooms was a gym, the other was an office. Either one would take some work to transform into a bedroom.

"It's your bedroom. I can sleep on the couch or go back to…"

"No," my husband nearly shouted at me. "I mean, I'd prefer if you stayed. We can't really figure things out if we never see one another."

"That's true, but I don't think it's right to take your bedroom. It's your house."

"It's our house, Court. We're married and I invited you to live here with me as my wife. We might sleep in separate spaces until we figure out if you want to remain my wife, or whatever else we need to work through, but this is your house too. I need to know you're comfortable and that you have a private space to get away from me, if you need it."

"And what about your private space?"

"I can go in my office or work out my frustrations in the gym until I get some things moved around."

"Flynn, I don't want this to be the end of us."

"Well, that sounds like a really good place to start. When you're sure, and you're ready to have a conversation about the future, you let me know and we'll work on what it takes to get there - together. Unless you don't want us to do it together," he reluctantly tacked on at the end.

Chapter Eighteen

COURTNEY

I WASN'T sure what to make of things. It had been a little over two weeks since Flynn moved out of his own bedroom to give me space to work through everything. It felt as though it should have taken longer for me to figure out what I wanted. In all honesty, I knew before I walked away from my husband and went to hide in his bedroom that day. The thought of walking away from him hurt me in a way that Beckett pushing me away never did.

That realization brought on a whole slew of issues, though. How was I supposed to trust myself, my judgement, or perception of things when I'd been so wrong - for so long - about Beckett? I agreed to marry that man and I had no problem living across town from him while we were together. I couldn't imagine not living with Flynn.

That wasn't entirely true. I didn't have to imagine it, because although we shared a house, we were rarely in it at the same time. If we were, it was usually when we were asleep in separate rooms. I'd never felt lonelier in my life than I had the past two weeks without Flynn's big presence to fill the empty spaces. I had always loved and respected him, but I was beginning to think that my feelings for my husband ran much deeper than that. If only he were around for me to tell him.

"You look lost."

I startled and turned to see Hadley standing in the door of my classroom. "Sorry, I didn't realize you were there."

"Obviously. What's on your mind, bestie?" If only my sigh could be translated into words. "Still living in an icebox at home?"

Okay, maybe my best friend could translate my sighs. "Yep."

"Have you tried to approach him? He told you he wanted to respect you enough to give you space to work through things."

"It's hard to approach him when he's never around."

"What do you mean?"

"I only know he's been home to sleep because things are moved around by the time I wake up in the morning. Otherwise, it's like I'm living in that house on my own."

"You guys don't even eat dinner together?" Hadley's shock made me feel even worse about the situation. It wasn't normal, even for two people who supposedly needed a little space to figure things out.

"You don't think he's hooking up with other women, since you two aren't really a couple, do you?"

"I didn't until now. What do you mean we're not really a couple?"

"It seems like you went back to the marriage being just an arrangement." Hadley shrugged her shoulders as if to say it was pretty obvious to her and should have been to me.

"Oh my God! Is that what we've done? That's not what I wanted."

"Maybe he thought you decided your marriage was in name only, since you've basically kept to yourself. Did you two ever discuss what your arrangement would look like before the wedding?"

"Not really. I assumed we would have a normal marriage, or as close to one as possible under the circumstances."

"But you never clarified that you were supposed to remain exclusive and not have hookups with other people while you were married for convenience's sake?"

I wanted to strangle her. "Why didn't you bring up these questions before I said, 'I do'? I thought we would both live up to the vows we took. What if he's been screwing other people? Do I even have the right to be angry about it?"

"Of course, you do. I'm sorry, bestie. I didn't mean to send you into a tailspin." Hadley sighed and then offered me a pitiful version of a smile. "It's half day, and you don't have another class. Why don't you take off and go have a conversation with your husband?"

"I'm supposed to stick around and do planning and enter the kids' grades into the system."

Hadley gave me a look that said she knew better. "We both know you have already done those things, so stop being a coward and go figure out where you stand with your husband. If nothing else, you deserve to know if he thinks you have an open relationship right now." She turned to leave, but I heard her as she muttered, "Can't believe you didn't think that one through before it smacked you in the face."

The sad reality was that I could believe it. Hadn't I been just as willfully blind when it came to Beckett? Maybe there was something in the Robeson genetics that made me completely stupid and blind to the world in their presence. There really was no other explanation for why I seemed to lose my mind and forget the important things or overlook the obvious things that should have tripped my red flag triggers.

I grabbed my bag, locked up my classroom, and took off to the parking lot without giving it another thought. Once I was in my car, I noticed the time and the grumble of my stomach let me know it was lunch time as well. I pulled into my favorite deli and grabbed some food and a couple of drinks to take with me. If nothing else, maybe Flynn and I could have lunch together and at least set a time to talk about the important stuff after the work day concluded for him.

JEFF WASN'T at his desk when I got off the elevator on my husband's floor. His office took up the entire floor of one of the few high-rise buildings in our downtown area. It felt a little too big city to me, considering we didn't even live or work in Atlanta. Still, I plastered a smile on my face and marched past the reception area where Jeff would normally be stationed and straight down the hallway that led to my husband's office and several conference rooms.

As I got closer, a woman's voice rang out loud and clear and set off alarm bells in my mind. No. He wouldn't be carrying on an affair at the office, would he?"

When I drew near and saw the blinds to his office were opened, the threat of seeing him engaged in a sexual encounter with another woman subsided. Then, I heard something that set my nerves on fire. My husband laughed. When I got close enough to be able to see inside his office, his head was tipped back and his throat worked with the movement.

The worst part was, there was a gorgeous blonde perched on a chair that had been pulled around so close to his own that their arms touched as they moved. It was only then that I noticed they had take-out containers spread all over his desk.

He was having a cozy lunch with a woman who looked at him as though he hung her own personal moon in the sky. The empty feeling in the pit of my stomach was back and it was all my fault. Hadley had been right. If I hadn't been such a damn coward, I wouldn't be standing in the hallway watching my husband and another woman look so damn comfortable with each other. He laughed again and my heart sunk right into that gnawing void in my stomach. He seemed happy with her. I had barely seen my husband in weeks, and when I did, he certainly wasn't smiling, let alone laughing in such a carefree way.

I turned and walked back toward the front of the office before either of them noticed me lurking. When I got to the front desk, the weight of the deli bag in my hand finally registered and I tossed it in the trash beside the front desk along with our two drinks. He wouldn't miss the lunch I brought, considering he had one of his own with a woman who made him happier than I ever had.

Chapter Nineteen

FLYNN

KYLIE WAS ALWAYS a breath of fresh air when she stopped in, and I was thankful for the lunch she brought considering I hadn't eaten at all that day. Still, something about her being there made me slightly uncomfortable. I couldn't put my finger on it until Jeff barged into my office.

His brows nearly flew into his perfectly-styled hairline as he took in the way Kylie and I sat together on one side of my desk. It was then I realized just how close she was to me. I scooted my chair to the left a bit and sent a pointed look Jeff's way.

This isn't what it looks like.

If only he could read my mind. Then again, I didn't know why I had to justify my actions to my assistant. The only person I would need to do that with was the wife who avoided me. That wasn't fair, I had been doing my own share of avoidance over the past couple of weeks too. In my defense, I wanted her to have to come to me.

"I was going to ask why you threw your whole deli lunch away in my trash, but I guess I got my answer," Jeff announced, and I didn't miss the tone he took. My assistant was not happy to see me in such an intimate position with a woman who was not my wife. He had been rooting for me to fix things with Courtney and clearly got the wrong impression about what was happening.

"I didn't have a deli lunch. I probably would have worked straight through again if Kylie hadn't brought lunch by, in the hopes of bribing me into a work lunch."

"What exactly are you working on?" Jeff asked. "Kung Pow and Kisses?"

"Jeff!" His name sounded more like a reprimand. He knew better than to get an attitude with clients.

"What would your wife think if she walked in here and saw how you conduct business?"

"Wife?" Kylie asked.

"That's about enough," I growled at my assistant, who apparently had a lightbulb moment as I was about to send him home for the day.

"Oh no!" he called out and then ran from my office. I could feel the panic in his voice and took off after him. When I got to the front desk, it was to see Jeff pull a bag from Court's favorite deli out of the trash, along with two sodas.

"Where did that come from?" Even as I asked the question, I feared the answer.

"Her name is on the receipt," Jeff confirmed.

"Fuck."

"I can only imagine what she saw when she stopped by to bring you lunch. Considering Kylie was about hair's breadth from crawling into your lap when I walked in."

Again, Jeff's tone was admonishing at best, downright accusatory would have been a better description.

"Nothing was going on."

"Nothing to you or would it have looked like something to your wife?"

"Flynn?" I turned to see Kylie headed down the hall toward us. "Did I hear Jeff correctly? He said you were married. Since when?"

"I am married," I informed her for the first time. It wasn't because I tried to hide the fact. I simply didn't think it mattered since I had no interest in Kylie outside of business.

"You're not wearing a ring."

"No, I'm not." I stared down at my hand and remembered that the one thing we hadn't managed to get done before our wedding was to procure a ring. Like hell was I going to wear the one that had been made for my cousin, even though his mother offered to loan it to me until I could get one of my own.

"That woman earlier," she whispered.

"What woman?" I already knew who she was talking about, but I hadn't noticed my wife and didn't think Kylie had seen anyone either.

"There was a woman standing outside your office earlier. I saw her briefly and then she disappeared. I thought it was just one of your employees who didn't want to disturb you, since you had a lunch date."

"I didn't have a lunch date," I snapped.

"No, I guess in your mind, you didn't," Kylie agreed. "I'm really sorry. I thought…" She hesitated a moment and then came right out with it. "We've worked so well together in the past, and I've always admired you. I thought I would take a chance and shoot my shot."

I stared at her for a moment. It had been completely lost on me that she had been trying to hint at something more than a working relationship between us.

"Seems like you're still trying to shoot your shot even after finding out that Flynn is married," Jeff snapped at her. Kylie stepped back and threw her hand over her mouth as she gasped in shock. She had all but forgotten my assistant was there to witness her declare her intentions.

"No, I wouldn't. Oh my God." She took off toward the elevator without looking back.

"Fuck!" I yelled as Jeff stood there staring off at the elevator with a sour expression that pulled the corners of his mouth down in a frown.

"I would wish you good luck explaining this to your wife, but I'm not sure you deserve it."

"I swear to you, everything was innocent on my end," I told my assistant.

He gave me a look that could be defined as the embodiment of sarcasm before he rolled his eyes at me. "That much was obvious from the sheer obliviousness you exhibited with Kylie just now. I'm not the one you need to convince, though."

Jeff was right. I had some serious work to do to make my wife understand she hadn't walked in on what she most likely thought she had. I ran back to my office and pulled up the security feed. I emailed the clip of Kylie and me in my office as well as what just went down at the front desk to myself, so I would have it to show Courtney. Then, I went back and watched the video of my wife as she walked off the elevator and came down the hallway. She stood there and watched us for a few minutes before she finally turned to leave with a hurt look on her face.

Dammit, she had been smiling as she approached my office. She was obviously at a turning point, and had come to a decision about things, only for my visit from Kylie to mess it all up before I even knew my wife was there.

I left the office and headed home to go explain things, but when I got there, Courtney wasn't there. I called, texted, and got no response. The only recourse I had was to suck up my pride and call the people closest to her. I dialed Hadley first, considering that was who my wife ran to last time. As soon as she picked up, she screamed into the phone.

"Fuck you, Robeson. I was on your side but now you can go choke on a disease infected dick!"

"Please, Hadley it wasn't..." I didn't get to finish because she hung up on me. I tried to call Reed after that.

"Let me guess," my father-in-law sighed into the phone. "You lost my daughter again."

"I know it seems like a habit, but I promise it's not."

"See that it doesn't become one. Two times in as many weeks isn't a great track record though, Flynn."

"I understand that. Do you know-"

He cut me off. "Hadley."

"That was my first call. She told me to choke on a disease infected dick and then hung up."

Reed whistled down the line. "I don't know what you did, but good luck with that." It sounded like he was about to hang up on me too, and then he came back with, "And Flynn, if my daughter needs help to bury a body, it's nothing personal." Once that message was delivered, he hung up on me too.

"Fuck!"

I knew, without a doubt, that my wife was with her best friend. As much as I wanted to run to her, apologize, and explain the situation, it felt like the right thing to do was to give her a little time to calm down first. At the very least, I needed enough time to figure out how to get around her bulldog of a best friend because there was no way Hadley would open her door to me if she thought I had been cheating on Courtney.

<hr>

BY THE TIME midnight rolled around, I knew my wife didn't have any plans to come home. I sent her one more text, just in case she decided to look at it.

> Flynn: I'm sorry. As cliche as this sounds, it wasn't what it looked like. I have video of the office before and after you left, if it makes a difference.I promise you there was nothing going on between me and Kylie. She was there for a work a lunch- at least on my end anyway. Please, come home so I can explain.

Not that I thought I would get one, but after thirty minutes, my text still went unanswered.

Forty-five minutes later, after I'd finally hung Courtney's canvases in my living room, my cell started to ring. I dove for it and just barely hit the button on the fourth ring.

"Hello?"

At first, I didn't hear anything other than the din of a bunch of voices and music in the background.

"Hello?" I questioned again. "Courtney?"

"My hubby-and…" I heard her say, but it didn't sound like she was speaking to me.

"Hey man," a man's voice came over the line. "I think I have your wife here. She's pretty fucked up and lost her friend in the crowd." My heart pounded erratically in my chest at the thought of how dangerous Courtney's situation was. She was relying on a strange man for her safety and didn't even realize.

"Where are you?" he rattled off a bar name and the relative location. "I'll be there in ten minutes. Don't let her out of your sight."

"No worries, man. If it was my sister or wife, I would hope that someone else would look out for her. I'll be here and make sure she doesn't wander." He chuckled. "Not that it would be possible, she's practically asleep standing up."

"Fucking hell," I murmured into the phone as I grabbed my wallet and keys and headed for my car.

"I'll stay on the line with you, if it will make you feel better."

"Yeah, it would. Thanks again for doing this."

"Like I said, no worries. Happy to help."

"Id dat my hubby-and?" I heard Courtney slur.

"Yes, ma'am."

"Done fink he likes meh."

"I promise you that he does," the man told her.

"Okay," she drew the word out in what amounted to a long sigh as the stranger who was looking out for her laughed.

"How about you sit down right here, darlin'?"

"Nuf glab a whuff." Whatever she tried to say was clearly not in English. "Hashes... Haddddd...Had-leeee?"

"Any clue what all that translates to?" the man asked me.

"Hadley is her best friend, and probably who was with her tonight."

"Ah, I see. Pretty sure the girl she was with is fucking my friend in the bathroom."

"Jesus," I hissed.

"No judgement, man."

"Let me guess, you were supposed to hook up with my wife?"

"Nah. Not my style. Clocked her ring immediately, and besides, she told me she was married about thirty times before that last shot caught up to her."

I pulled up into the parking lot of the bar that was in what looked like a mini strip mall. "Of all the places," I groaned. It was a fucking biker bar. The man on the phone laughed once again.

"Like I said, no worries, your wife was safe the whole night."

I walked into the bar and scanned the area. It took a minute, but I finally found her slumped over in a half-sized booth on the back wall. I hung up with the guy who was keeping an eye on her and made my way to them.

He stood as soon as I got to them. "Sorry to worry you with the call, but I know my buddy, and her friend was pretty shitfaced. They'll be at it all night and her friend won't remember her until she sobers up some."

"Thanks. Hadley and I will have a conversation about

that shit once she sobers up, too. If you don't mind, could you go get her for me while I get my wife out to the car?"

"I'm not so sure how that will go over," the man hedged.

"Don't really care. I appreciate you looking out for my wife, but her friend is my responsibility too. Court would never forgive me if I left Hadley behind, especially if she's as drunk as you made her sound."

The man threw his hands up. "I get it, but they made their hook up plans long before the alcohol was involved."

"They?" I questioned, wondering if Courtney had planned to hook up with someone too.

"My buddy, Trace, and your wife's friend," he clarified and then smiled a little too sweetly at my woman. "Told you, she informed me - and everyone else who tried to talk to her - that she was a married woman and took those vows seriously."

I had to smile at that. My beautiful girl was loyal to a fault, even when she thought I wasn't. That was something we would clear up as soon as she sobered up though. Before we could say anything else, I noticed Hadley stumble out from a hallway toward the opposite corner from the booth. At least she had the presence of mind to look upset when she didn't immediately see my wife somewhere.

The minute our eyes met, she stumble-ran toward me. "Oh my God! Where is she?"

"She's fine, she's safe." I pointed to the booth where Courtney had slumped all the way over on the seat and started to snore. I grinned down at her and shook my head. "Your friend here took care of her until I could get here." Even in her inebriated state, Hadley winced at the tone of my voice. "She's lucky he was a good guy."

Hadley sniffed and then tears tracked down her face. "I'm so sorry," she said, but it came out so low that I almost missed it.

"Come on, man. I'll help you guys out to your car."

"Thanks…" I left the gratitude hanging as I waited for him to fill in his name.

"Call me Sparks."

"Sparks?" I asked.

"Yep." He tapped the spot over his chest where his name was represented on a patch.

"Thanks again, Sparks. Appreciate you looking out for my woman."

"I'd say any time, but hopefully, you keep her on a shorter leash next time." He winked at me to let me know he was teasing, but Hadley must have missed that.

"My friend is snot a dog!" Her words jumbled a bit, but nowhere near as bad as Courtney's had before she passed out. I lifted my wife into my arms and allowed Sparks to lead the way, so he could open doors for us. When we got to the car, I laid Courtney across the backseat and put Hadley up front with me.

My wife didn't stir once until after I made sure Hadley got up to her apartment okay. It sucked that I couldn't go up and double-check that she had everything locked up properly, but I also wouldn't risk leaving my passed-out wife in the car. Hadley called me once she was safely tucked into her apartment.

"Everything locked up?" I asked her.

"Yes, daddy!" She snickered at her own joke. "Wait, that felt gross. Can't say that to my bestie's hubby."

"I'm taking off. Are you sure you're okay?" I asked.

"Yep, but you won't be if you don't pull your head out of your butthole. She was never devastated over losing Beckett.

I took her at her word and headed home with my wife.

"Feel for ju."

"What's that?" I asked as Courtney mumbled.

"Fell in looove," she sang the last word in a long drawn out, very off-key note.

"You fell in love?" I questioned.

"Yep!"

"Was it with Sparks from the bar?" I asked. If she said yes, I might have thrown myself out of my own moving car.

"My hubb-and." Her answer made me grin, not that she could see it with her face buried in the leather seat. She had never told me that she loved me before. While they were a drunk woman's words, I still held onto them tightly.

"Love him," she managed to mumble again.

"He loves you too," I told her.

"Yeah?"

"Positive," I answered. Before I could say more, I heard her snort before she started to snore again. "I was just about to call you sweetheart, but with that loud-ass snore, we might need to search for some butch biker names for you instead."

Chapter Twenty

COURTNEY

I WAS PRETTY sure God hated me.

There was no other reason to feel like I'd been run over by a truck only to have a cat take a shit in my mouth. I tried to lick my lips because they were so dry, but my god-awful hungover death breath offended me as I opened my mouth. I groaned and the pillow beneath my head jiggled.

Wait.

That wasn't right.

I touched my pillow with my hand and quickly realized it was a human body, and if I wasn't mistaken a very manly human body. "No," I whispered. I would never forgive myself, and Flynn would probably never forgive me either for going home with another man.

Despite how much it hurt to see him so chummy with that woman in his office; after thinking about it, I had already come to the conclusion that there was most likely nothing going on between them. If there had been, his office door wouldn't have been wide open, nor would his blinds. Did it bother me that another woman was so close to my husband and he looked happy to have her there in his space? Yes. Did that mean he was cheating on me? No.

While it was a sucky situation for me, waking up in bed with a man was way worse, especially since I was only in a bra and panties. At least I wasn't totally nude. I wasn't stupid though. There were exactly zero circumstances where a husband would be okay with his wife waking up in her undies while draped across a naked - or nearly naked - man.

I cracked my eye open and noticed a little scar right under the man's nipple. I damn near heaved a sigh of relief. Flynn had that scar. It was his body I used as a pillow. I wanted to leap up and jump for joy that I hadn't completely annihilated any chance of making my marriage work, but the minute I started to shift, my tummy rocked and rolled in the worst possible way.

I jumped up and stumble-ran to the bathroom just in time to try out for a lead role in a remake of The Exorcist. Whatever demon crawled in my body through the numerous shots I took the night before wanted out in an explosive way.

My throat felt raw as tears tracked down my cheeks. Every time I thought there was no way there could possibly be anything else in my stomach, my body worked to prove me wrong. I was fairly certain that my organs were liquifying and purging because there was no other explanation for the volume of vomit I spewed.

"Be gone, demon," I whimpered as someone grabbed my hair and pulled it back into a half ponytail, half bun type thing.

"Demons, huh?" Flynn asked. There was no judgement in his tone as he stepped back to give me some space.

"Sorry. It was a rough night."

"I know."

"What do you mean, you know?"

"I'm the one who brought you home." I turned my head to the side and looked at my gorgeous husband as he stood there in nothing but his boxer briefs and ran a washcloth under the faucet. "Got a call from you." He stopped and thought about that for a minute. "Well, I think you started the call and got sidetracked, so this man picked up your phone and told me where I could find you."

I crinkled my brow in confusion. "A man?"

Flynn brought the rag over to me and after I wiped my face clean with it, he rinsed it out and then ran it under cool water before he placed it on the back of my neck. "It will help," he said to stop me from removing it. Then he told me all about the parts of my night I hadn't been coherent enough to remember.

"I could have been hurt."

"Yeah, you could have, but I think everyone learned a lesson about that last night."

"Are you sure Hadley was okay?" I didn't know why I wanted to cry. Flynn had been placed in a bad situation the night before, or maybe earlier this morning. It sucked that he had to make the decision between staying with me or checking to be sure my friend was secure. I understood why I would be his priority, but it didn't stop me from worrying about my bestie.

"I talked to her about an hour ago."

"She was awake already?"

"Yes, she called me to make sure you were doing okay, since you weren't answering her calls. She feels a good bit of guilt for leaving you alone to pass out with a stranger while she hooked up with his friend."

"I'm a grown up. It's not her job to babysit me," I grumbled.

"Speaking of being a grown up," my husband mentioned. "Please, don't ever do that again. You were at a biker bar. If you hadn't been sitting with the one decent guy in that bar, things could have turned out very differently, Court."

I nodded, too afraid of my own overwhelming emotions to say anything in my defense. Truthfully, there was no defending the fact that I got that drunk in a place I wasn't familiar with while surrounded by strangers. I don't think I even registered that we were at a biker bar because my feelings after seeing my husband cozy with another woman blinded me to everything else.

"You wanna talk about why you were there in the first place?" Flynn asked.

"Not really," I murmured.

"I think we should. It's not doing us any good to keep going in this cone of silence the way we have been."

"I've barely seen you," I argued. "It's hard to talk to someone who isn't there."

"You're right. That was my fault. At first, I wanted to give you time to work through whatever you needed, but then I was afraid that in working through everything, you would decide to leave me."

"We're a mess." I groaned when my stomach heaved again like I might throw up some more. Flynn took one look at me and backed toward the door.

"I'm going to grab some Ginger soda and crackers for

you. Maybe it will help settle your stomach." He was gone before I could argue that there was no way I would ever put food or liquid in my body again after puking up an entire ocean of alcohol a few minutes ago.

When my husband came back, he helped me to our bed and tucked me in before he handed me the soda and left the crackers on the bedside table.

"Why are you being so nice to me?"

"You're my wife, Court, for better or worse, remember?"

"We both know this marriage is a sham."

"It's not a sham. Not to me, anyway."

I patted the bed next to me and Flynn climbed in and got under the covers with me. "Can we stay here all day?"

"I think that would probably be best until you're ready to try some real food." I chuckled at his answer but cut it short when it made me feel queasy. "Thank you for coming to get me and taking care of me."

"It was my fault you were in that state to begin with."

"Don't," I told him. "There's no need to make excuses for what I did. You are right when you said it could have gone bad. I was so messed up emotionally that I didn't even realize I was in a biker bar, and that was before the I ever drank the first shot."

Flynn reached for his phone and queued up a video. "I wanted you to be able to see this." I took it and saw what happened after I left his office the other day. I had to laugh at his cluelessness, but inside I secretly cheered Jeff on. He was a real girl's guy.

"You should give Jeff a raise."

"I'm sure he would appreciate that, considering I nearly fired him for insinuating things that weren't true."

"They looked true from where I was standing."

"It has been brought to my attention that I may have also had a moment of cluelessness where my situation was concerned. I've worked with Kylie in the past and there has never been a time where I crossed a line with her. It's been one of my rules since I took over my grandfather's business when he passed. I don't sleep with clients." He coughed and then looked me in the eye. "And that was a rule before I was married. Afterward, the rule was amended to: 'I don't sleep with anyone but my wife.'"

I chuckled at that. "Good call, Mister."

"I need you to know that I was never interested in her."

"I had a moment of drunken clarity where I knew it wasn't what it looked like, but it still hurt to see you carefree and laughing with someone else when I could barely catch a glimpse of you, let alone see you smile or laugh or look happy to be near me."

"Court," Flynn whispered. "I have only seemed miserable because I couldn't be around you lately. I promised to give you space until you sorted things and were ready to talk about what you wanted. I didn't want to trample on that space, but it was killing me to keep my distance."

"Let's not do the space thing anymore," I suggested.

"Are you sure?"

"Positive."

I WAS fine when I woke up, especially since Flynn once again acted as my pillow. I could get used to sleeping with him again, if I wasn't careful. It took me a minute, in my sleepy state, to realize we had already decided to work on being a couple. With any luck, I would get used to it.

Flynn shifted beneath me, and it dislodged me just enough from his chest that I had to adjust my position. Unfortunately, when I tried to do that, I was hit with an echo of the nausea I had the day before. I stayed still for a minute and willed it to pass, but then Flynn turned fully onto his side and bounced the bed just enough that I couldn't hold back.

I jumped and ran to the bathroom in a panic and barely made it to the toilet before I threw up whatever was left on my stomach from dinner last night. It wasn't much, mostly stomach bile, but that didn't stop my body from heaving like it was purging hangover demons from my body again.

"What the hell?" I groaned miserably as a pair of hands worked to pull my hair back from me again.

"I hate to break it to you sweetheart, but hangovers don't last two whole days."

"Maybe I was never really hung over and I caught a stomach bug."

"Oh, no, you were definitely hung over judging by how drunk you were the other night. You might be right about the stomach bug though."

"I'm sorry"

"Why are you apologizing?"

"I'm apologizing in advance for when it's you with your head in the toilet. I've wrapped myself around you both nights."

"I don't mind that one bit."

"You will when you're heaving your guts up because I got my disgusting cooties all over you."

"Nothing about you is disgusting, not even your cooties." When I threw him a dubious look, the jerk laughed at me. "We're newlyweds, so everything is still in the 'she's so cute' stage."

"Great, let me know when that changes, so I can keep my gross stuff to myself."

He laughed again as he left the bathroom. "I'll grab you a Ginger soda and some crackers to help settle your stomach."

It was an echo of what he had said to me the day before, only it hit a little differently when I wasn't hungover. "It can't be..." I whispered to myself before I dragged my ass back to the bed in search of the phone I had on the charger. I dialed Hadley and as soon as she said, 'Hello', my words came spewing out at the same exorcist rate my vomit did.

"Do you remember when Sarah came down with something in our junior year?"

"Yeah, it was pregnancy. She came down with pregnancy, Courtney."

"Yeah, but before she knew that part, we thought she had the flu or food poisoning or something and the only thing that made her feel better was..."

"Ginger Ale and Saltine Crackers," Hadley answered with a laugh. "I remember. What made you think of that?"

"That's what Flynn got me for my hangover yesterday."

"Aww that was sweet of him."

"It's also what he got me this morning for the tummy bug I must have because I threw up like I was hung over all over again."

Hadley didn't say a word as we both processed exactly

what I was getting at. When she finally did speak, it was to ask the question I hadn't been able to say out loud.

"Is it possible that you're pregnant?"

"If I am, it was our wedding night, or I guess any time in that first week or so when we..." I cut myself off because I wasn't one to talk about my intimate moments with my friend.

"Did you use protection?"

"All except for that first night."

"Courtney!"

"It was my wedding night and neither of us were really thinking about safety."

"Well, it sounds like you need a doctor's appointment and a couple conversations with Flynn. Do you need me to run to the store and grab a couple tests for you in the meantime?"

"Would you?"

"That's what BFFs are for."

"I love you forever!"

She blew a kiss at me and hung up as I stared off into space and wondered what Flynn's reaction would be.

Chapter Twenty-One

FLYNN

AFTER I OVERHEARD my wife's side of the conversation with her friend, I backtracked to the kitchen to give the news time to sink in. Was it the best time for her to get pregnant? Probably not.

If she's pregnant, then I get to keep her forever.

The voice in my head was full of excitement at the prospect, for several reasons, but the main one was that we would be bound together with a connection she never had with Beckett. No matter what, we would be in one another's lives from that point on. It gave us more incentive to make the most of our marriage. So, even though it was unexpected, unplanned, and crappy timing considering we were only just working out the details of our relationship, I was fucking ecstatic over the possibility that we made a baby together.

I took the Ginger Ale and crackers to Courtney after we both had a few minutes to process. Her smile was awkward as she thanked me for taking care of her again.

"I will always be here to take care of you, sweetheart."

"I might just hold you to that," she whispered.

"Please do." I turned and got ready to leave. "I'm going to clean up our mess from yesterday. Do you need anything else?"

Courtney shook her head and then plastered a fake as fuck smile on her face. "Hadley is going to drop by in a bit with a thermometer and some other stuff."

I wanted to laugh at her blatant lie. I took a step closer and held my arm out. "Do you have a fever? I can check to see if you're warm."

"No!" Did she realize I could hear how desperate she sounded to keep me at a distance? It took everything in me not to laugh. "I mean, we might as well wait until I can get an accurate temperature, that way I don't get ahead of myself and end up at the Urgent Care."

"Okay, yell if you need me. I'll let Hadley in when she gets here, so you don't have to get up."

"Thanks," Courtney called out to me as I left our bedroom. It was a good thing I already overheard their conversation, because my wife was horrible with subterfuge.

The minute I opened the door for Hadley she waved and ran straight for the bedroom. I walked that way to see what they would say, but by the time I got there, they were already in the bathroom. I moved to the door and knocked.

"Are you okay? Getting sick again?" I asked.

"Um, yeah. Hadley's here with me. I'll be okay."

"Okay, well I'm not far, if you need me."

"Thanks, Flynn."

"Yeah, thanks to the Hubsters, now go away. Women don't like men to hear them puke."

"I heard it yesterday," I called back to her. My wife wasn't puking, though. I could hear her peeing.

"Go away," Hadley yelled through the door.

"And this morning. I even pulled her hair back both times," I called out to her. I could have left but it was more fun to fuck with them, since they wanted to try to keep my wife's maybe pregnancy a secret.

"Maybe your Urgent Care idea was plausible," I pondered loudly.

"Flynn!" Courtney called out.

"Yes, Nemesis?"

"Can you please give me a minute?"

"Sure thing, sweetheart." I called back and that time I moved away from the bathroom door, but I wasn't about to go far. I wanted to see my wife's face first thing after she came out. I had forgotten all about the fact that we hadn't used protection on our wedding night, and we had fucked a lot. I pumped three loads in her before the sun came up.

I hoped like hell that meant she was for sure knocked up because if she wasn't, we were going to have to start trying with a purpose.

When they came out, both women seemed a bit shell-shocked. "Everything okay?" I asked. "Did you have a fever?"

Hadley continued to make her way to the bedroom door. "I'm gonna…" She tipped her head toward the door and then walked out without finishing that thought. I heard her leave the house before I turned my attention back to my wife, who had taken a seat beside me on the bed. She still hadn't found her voice, so I decided to take the burden off her shoulders.

"Is there any chance that it's Beckett's?" Courtney shook her head, but still didn't say anything. "How do you know?"

"We hadn't even had sex in two months." She choked out a dark laugh. "That probably should have told me something, huh? I thought it was just because we were both busy, stressed with the upcoming wedding, and... You probably don't want to hear all this," she finally said.

"I don't want to, but I think we both need to clear the air about a few things. What you're saying is that it would be obvious if you were pregnant with Beckett's kid. Right?"

"Yes. I would most likely be showing by now. I'm going to make an appointment with my doctor. They'll be able to verify if I really am pregnant and how far along."

"I'd like to be there, if you don't mind."

"I don't mind. If I am pregnant, it's most likely yours unless I'm having one of those weird pregnancies where the woman doesn't know, and I doubt that very much." When she stopped to look at me, it finally dawned on her that she didn't have to break the news to me. "How did you know?"

"I'm not as dumb as I look. I think I probably figured it out about the same time you did." I laughed as I thought about overhearing her conversation. My hand was on the doorknob, ready to turn it to enter our bedroom when it occurred to me that she had been sick two mornings in a row and for both of those mornings, I brought her the same things we kept on hand for the women who were pregnant in the office.

"Also, you and Hadley weren't exactly quiet about it when you called her, even though you were trying to be."

"You also don't seem angry," my wife pointed out.

"Why would I be?"

"We didn't exactly marry for love, Flynn."

"No, but what's to stop that from happening? I love you, always have," I admitted.

"Yeah, as friends," my wife corrected.

I shook my head once and then remembered she probably wasn't ready for the whole truth about my feelings just yet. "That's a better starting point than a lot of people have when they become parents. At least this wasn't a one-night stand with a stranger or…"

"A pregnancy with my maybe cheating ex-fiancé," she filled in as I winced.

"Yeah. That would suck," I agreed. "The thing is, we're already married. We're friends. We're working on our communication skills. By the time this little one gets here, we'll be a well-oiled machine at this relationship stuff."

"So, you *want* to have this baby?"

The way she emphasized the word "want" made me sit up and take notice. I hadn't even thought about the fact that she might not want to carry the pregnancy to term or be a mom. It wasn't something we had really talked about yet.

"If you want this baby, then I am in a million percent. If you don't, then I'll be okay with that because it's your body. You get to decide."

"What is your preference?" she asked.

I shook my head again. "My preference doesn't matter."

"It does, Flynn. This is our baby. If I really am pregnant, then it is both of ours."

I took my hand and placed it over hers where she had rested it on her belly as if to protect the very idea of what might be growing inside her. "I think you already made your decision," I told her softly, "and that's great because it aligns perfectly with what I want."

"Really?" she questioned as big tears formed in her eyes and spilled over.

I caught the first one with my fingertip before it could travel down her cheek. "Really, Nemesis. I can't think of any better news than starting a family with the one woman I trust to do the best damn job of parenting with me."

"Thank you," she whispered before she laid her head on my shoulder.

"Pretty sure I should be the one thanking you for being willing to bring my spawn into the world. Imagine what it will be like in a few years when your little vengeance demons start to curse us for running out of cookies."

Courtney's laughter made my fucking heart sing. It was like a dream come true. Not only was she finally mine, but she was also carrying my baby.

Chapter Twenty-Two

FLYNN

"It looks like your due date aligns perfectly with your suspected date of conception," the doctor told us as she moved the wand around on Courtney's belly. You're just about at the eight-week mark now, and listen." She hit a button on the machine and a fast-paced whooshing noise came through the speakers.

"Is that?" my wife asked. Tears formed in her eyes as she looked back at me after the doctor nodded her head. "Our baby's heartbeat, Flynn."

"Yeah, sweetheart, I caught that." I tried to choke back the emotion in my own voice. The baby had been this idea, an object that was beyond comprehension because it was out of sight. Somehow, hearing the heartbeat did more to make it real than anything else.

"That's our baby," Courtney blubbered as her eyes moved back to the screen. I wanted to look too, but I couldn't take my eyes off my wife. When I glanced over at the doctor, she was watching me with a big smile on her face.

"I'll get some pictures printed off for you. There will be a prescription for a good prenatal vitamin at the counter when you check out. You can opt for one that is over the counter, but I really like this one because you get more of the vitamins mom and baby need and less of the extra junk that they don't."

"Then that's what we'll get," I assured her.

After the doc left us alone in the room, I helped Courtney wipe all the goop off her belly. "We're probably lucky she was able to see the baby this way."

"What way?"

"With the wand on my belly."

"Is there another way?" I asked because I honestly didn't know. I thought all sonograms were done with some gel splashed on the belly and the little wand pushing uncomfortably on someone's bladder. That's what all the pregnant women I had ever known led me to believe anyway.

"Yep, in the early stages of pregnancy, they usually have to do a transvaginal ultrasound."

"Trans-vag- Is that what I think it is?" I asked, almost horrified to think that they might have shoved what amounted to a camera up my wife's pussy.

"Yes, it means they stick a condom on a wand and insert it inside a woman to see the baby."

"It's for the best that they didn't have to do it that way, sweetheart."

Courtney chuckled and then held her hands out to me, so I could help her down from the table. "I guess this makes it official. We're going to be parents."

I pulled her into a hug and didn't even want to let go.

"What would you say if I asked you to go out on a dinner date with me tonight?"

My wife grinned up at me. "We're married, Flynn. You don't have to ask me out on a date."

"That's where you're wrong. We've never really gone out on a date before because we got married first. I think we need to have a designated date night at least once a week until the baby gets here and then again after he or she is a few months old. I don't want you to ever feel like you're not a priority to me. You are and we need to keep a healthy balance in our lives."

"Best to start the habit now, huh?" she teased.

"Exactly. So, what do you say? Are you feeling up to dinner?" I glanced down at the time on my phone as we walked to the reception desk to make Courtney's next appointment and pick up her prescription.

"As long as we can go within the next hour or so. I'm starving."

"We can go whenever you'd like."

WE HAD ONLY JUST SAT DOWN and ordered our drinks when the waitress came back to our table and smiled as she started to pour from a bottle of wine neither of us ordered. Courtney couldn't even drink it, for obvious reasons.

"We didn't order wine," I reminded the woman, thinking she had the wrong table.

"Oh, no. It was a gift from…"

"Stephie, please come help!" A frantic woman called out

as our waitress turned her way. She glanced across the room and groaned audibly.

"Not again!" She set the bottle of wine on the table along with the one glass she managed to pour, and took off with a quick, "So sorry, I'll be right back."

"Well, I guess the wine will remain a mystery for now." Courtney giggled as she picked up the bottle and stared longingly at the label. "It was Satan," she announced.

"What was Satan?"

"The one who sent our table a bottle of wine. It had to be Satan. Who else would send my favorite wine when I can't drink it?"

I glanced around to see if I noticed anyone familiar, but no one stood out. Courtney picked up the filled glass, but I stopped her before she could take a sip. "You can't, remember?"

"I was only going to sniff it. Can't I just…" She held it up to her nose and closed her eyes as she took in the delightful scent of tropical fruits and honeysuckle.

When I got it back from her, I also scented some sort of spice mixed in with the rest. My wife watched every move I made as I sipped the rich white wine.

"I can see why it's your favorite.

"You don't like wine, do you?"

"I don't dislike it." She smirked at my answer.

"You prefer to drink liquor or beer, though," Courtney encouraged.

"Honestly, I don't have an alcohol preference because I rarely drink."

"Wait, seriously?"

"I don't dislike it." My wife smirked at my answer.

"You prefer to drink liquor or beer though." It was a statement, not a question, but I felt the need to correct her assumptions, since we needed to do better about getting to know one another.

"Honestly, I don't have an alcohol preference because I rarely drink."

"Are you kidding me?" she asked. When I gave her a non-verbal no, she asked, "How did I not know this? I always thought you were a partying playboy through college."

"No. I don't know why everyone assumed that. I spent a lot of time playing Designated Driver for friends, so maybe they assumed I was drinking with them."

"Huh."

"Is that a good 'huh' or a bad one?"

She laughed at me. "It's just a *learned something new about you* sound. It's good to know, though." Courtney stared at me thoughtfully for a few minutes and then grinned as if she had a secret. "You only had one glass of champagne at our wedding reception."

My cheeks burned red-hot at her proclamation. It was true, but I hadn't realized she had been paying such close attention. "Yes."

"It's weird that I only just now realized that, even though I watched you all night."

"You watched me all night, huh?"

"Well, you were my new husband. I was trying to figure you out."

"I'm not a stranger. You already know me."

"I knew you as a friend, not a husband. They're totally different."

I took another sip of the wine and looked back up to meet Court's eyes. "This reminds me of summer for some reason."

"It's the honeysuckle. It always makes me think of sitting on a porch swing and watching kids play before a barbecue kicks off or a relaxing summer night out in the field stargazing."

"One day soon, you'll be able to watch the kids play from a porch swing." My house didn't have the swing, but it did have a wrap-around porch, so I hatched a plan to make sure she got one, so when next summer came, she could sit out there with me and have a glass of wine as we tended to our son or daughter. They would be too young to play on their own in the yard by next summer, but those moments would come with time, and I couldn't wait to share them with her.

Chapter Twenty-Three

FLYNN

"Is it weird that we always leave these appointments and go straight to eat somewhere?" Courtney asked.

"No. You're pregnant. Feels like good planning to me." She laughed at my answer as I got her squared away in the car and walked around to the driver's side. "Are you sure you're up to dinner with my family tonight?"

Courtney couldn't answer right away since she was mid-yawn. "We need to tell them, so it seems like the perfect time since your sisters will be there too."

I held the ultrasound photos in my hand before I tucked them in my pocket with my phone. "At least we'll have the fresh images to show everyone."

"Do you think they'll be excited?"

"My mom is going to lose her damn mind," I assured her. Courtney glowed as a beautiful smile spread across her sweet face. Maybe it was the pregnancy, or the excitement of finally being able to share our news, but whatever it was, it looked good on her.

"You are so beautiful," I told her before I turned my

attention back to getting the car started, so we could get to my parents' house in time for family dinner.

"Thank you." Her soft voice barely carried to me, as she looked away.

"I mean it."

"I know you do. I just don't understand how you could think so. I feel like a whale already."

"You can't even tell with that big-ass sweater on," I informed her, which made her laugh.

"See, it takes a big-ass sweater to hide all this and I am only four months along!" she whined.

"Do you hear me complaining?"

"No."

"Okay then. No one else's opinion matters."

I ignored the way she stared at me and grinned from ear-to-ear. It sucked that I had to focus my attention on driving, but I wouldn't risk an accident just to see her happiness aimed at me a bit longer.

When we got to the house, I was too busy helping my wife out of the car to notice that there was another vehicle in the driveway that shouldn't have been there. If I had been paying attention, we would have turned around and found a restaurant to go to for date night, rather than dinner with my family.

When my parents invited us that morning, I thought they had said it would be just us; my parents, two sisters, and then my wife and me. When Mom and Dad greeted us, I noticed the extra guests over their shoulders.

"I thought it was just the kids coming to dinner?"

My mom's face turned red with embarrassment as Gayle smiled softly and spoke up. "That's my fault, I'm afraid. We came to talk to your parents about something, and they invited us to join everyone for dinner. I hope you don't mind the intrusion." My aunt turned her attention from me to the woman at my side. "Courtney, it is so good to see you, my dear. You're looking absolutely radiant. What kind of skin care are you doing these days?"

My wife blushed and waved her off. "Nothing special," she managed to get out as my aunt and mom tutted her denials.

"To be young again and not even have to try to look good," my mom huffed as if she wasn't still in her prime.

"You're always effortlessly beautiful," Dad said to her. Every woman in the room swooned a bit, and I had to join Uncle Marty in rolling my eyes.

I glanced between Gayle and Marty then and noticed the distance between them. Normally, if we were all standing around, my uncle would have his arm around his wife in much the same way my dad always did with his. It struck me then that Marty had probably always emulated what he saw Dad do, because I didn't think he had it in him to be a sweet, caring husband of his own accord. Then again, I might have been prejudiced by the fact that I knew he was carrying on an affair with Courtney's mother.

That bitter pill was something else I had to contend with. I promised Reed that I wouldn't say anything until he collected all the information he would need in his divorce. He didn't want anyone to tip Jill off that he had hired a PI to follow her around. It sucked, because I didn't like keeping secrets from my wife, but I also knew my little Nemesis well enough to know that she would go after her mother for betraying her dad and ultimately their whole family dynamic.

My phone buzzed in my pocket, and when I went to pull it out to check my message, the ultrasound photos went fluttering to the floor. Just as that happened, the front door opened behind us and my fucking cousin marched in with a date in tow like he had every right.

"What's this?" Mom said as she bent to scoop up the ultrasound photos. My eyes darted between Mom with the pictures and my wife, whose face had gone ashen at the sight of Beckett.

"Is this what I think it is?" my mother shrieked in her excitement.

"Mom, shhh, we'll talk about it later."

Her eyes were bright and shining with joy as she ignored me and announced to the whole house, "I'm going to be a grandma!"

I quickly looked at Courtney, who had collected herself after the shock of seeing her former fiancé in my parents' home. She gave me a shoulder shrug and smirked as we watched my father lean in and study the images a little too closely.

"I guess the cat is out of the bag," Courtney stated as her arm wrapped around my waist and gave a reassuring squeeze.

"You're pregnant?" We both turned to see my cousin's eyes bouncing between the images in my parents' hands and Courtney. "Is that my baby? Did you think I wouldn't find out about it? Fuck you, Flynn! You can't claim my kid! I don't care if you won't divorce each other, you'll still have to deal with me. We'll have to coparent or whatever the fuck they call it. No, fuck that. You'll have to get a divorce. My kids won't be raised in a broken home, Courtney. We've loved one another our whole lives, we can work it out for our baby."

"Thank God the baby isn't yours." Courtney's shoulders sagged in obvious relief. "Coparent or whatever the fuck…" She muttered unhappily. Before anyone could say anything else, we all heard the slap of a hand on skin, and I turned to see that my cousin's date had nailed him right across the face.

"I can't believe you brought me to a family dinner and then had the nerve to propose to another woman."

"She's already my fiancée," Beckett argued.

"I'm married to his cousin," Courtney told the girl.

"So, you're a liar too?"

"No, I'm not. Babe. Look." Each word was punctuated with a heavy pause as he tried to find the right words and failed. "We were engaged and then she married my cousin to help him get his inheritance."

"Do you plan to get back with Beckett?" the girl asked my wife.

"God, no!" Courtney huffed. "Honestly, this whole conversation makes me want to vomit." She ignored everyone's open-mouthed stares and went to park her ass in the chair she dubbed, "the comfy one." I heard her sigh in relief as she took a load off.

"You are unbelievable Beckett Robeson. I thought you were bringing me to family dinner to make our relationship official."

"What relationship?" he asked her, and as sad it was, my cousin truly looked perplexed.

The woman slapped him again and then walked out. "Find your own ride home!" she yelled just before the door closed.

"How do you know it's not my baby?" Beckett asked my wife, as if his date hadn't just slapped him twice and left him.

Courtney rolled her eyes. "It's not your baby. I would be six months or more along for it to be yours and I'm only four months. Even if it had been yours, I wouldn't divorce Flynn or marry you. You've proven to be unreliable at best."

"We are in love with each other," he argued again.

"No, Beckett. We *were* in love. At least, I was. I'm not sure if you ever were. That love died the minute you tried to sell me off for a cabin and someone else filling our future children's college funds, so you wouldn't have to."

"Beckett!" Aunt Gayle hissed. Clearly, she hadn't known that he set everything in motion and basically tried to sell his fiancée to me for his own benefit. "Tell me that is not why you did this." When he didn't answer her, she fumed, but it was my uncle who spoke up next.

"I am truly disappointed in you, son. You deserve to see them happy and growing a family."

"You have no room to talk, Martin!" his wife sniped.

"Not here," Uncle Marty growled at her.

"Why not? Seems like the perfect time to air our dirty laundry." She turned to the rest of the gathered family. "Martin and I are getting a divorce. He's been cheating on me with…" She hesitated as her eyes flicked toward Courtney and then her cheeks heated. She must have realized how callous it would be to out the fact that Courtney's mother was having an affair.

"It's okay. I already know my mother is having an affair with him. My father told me this morning." My wife gave me a pointed look that I said I was only sort-of in trouble for not telling her myself.

"What the fuck?" Dad asked. "Marty, tell me you aren't that stupid. No offense, Courtney. It's not about your mom."

"None taken, even if it was," my Nemesis assured him.

The conversation devolved into a bunch of pointed fingers and accusations. Bea and Ky seemed to be enjoying the drama. Mina escaped without anyone else noticing. Mom grabbed a bottle of wine and mouthed "Sorry" to me. Dad looked ready to punch his brother, or his nephew, maybe both.

Finally, Courtney was the one to speak up as the voice of reason. "Okay, listen up!" she shouted above everyone else. "My husband and I have some amazing news to share with our family and we don't need whatever drama you guys have making that impossible. Please, take your arguments somewhere else."

"You can't kick me out of my brother's house," Marty insisted.

"She can, with my permission, but if I need to make it clear to you - go home, Marty. Take your son with you. Gayle, if you need to stay and chat with Margaret, feel free."

"You're letting my wife stay, but not me?" Marty asked.

"She didn't do anything wrong. She gets to stay. Now, brother, I asked you to leave. My daughter-in-law is pregnant and does not need all this added stress."

"She was supposed to be *my* daughter-in-law. That's supposed to be *my* grandchild!" Marty yelled.

"Maybe you should have taught our son to keep his dick in his pants where it belonged then," Gayle snapped at him. "Oh, never mind, you never learned that lesson either, so it was hard to pass on the knowledge."

"Gayle!" he cried out in shocked disbelief.

"Don't Gayle me. You've been sleeping with Courtney's mom for over a year! What if our son hadn't abandoned her for a profit? What if that was our grandchild and here you have made a mess of our lives. I was heartbroken that Courtney wouldn't be in our family as my daughter, but now I'm thankful. She doesn't have to bring a child into this world who will one day learn that her grandparents were adulterous assholes who ruined everything for everyone."

I cringed as my mom came and pulled Gayle away. My dad only grew angrier at his brother while Beckett made sad, puppy dog eyes at Courtney. She wasn't paying attention, though. She took advantage of everyone else being distracted and dug into my mom's peach cobbler that had been left unattended on the table. I thought about asking her to share but remembered what the doctor told us just a bit ago. My woman was eating for three, not two. She could have the whole damn cobbler to herself.

Chapter Twenty-Four

COURTNEY

"MY STOMACH KINDA HURTS," I complained as Flynn drove us home from the failed family dinner. "We didn't even get to tell them we're having twins," I pouted.

Flynn dropped his hand into my lap and squeezed my thigh. "We'll tell them another day when the news isn't overshadowed by all the drama from Aunt Gayle and Martin's divorce."

I chuckled. "It's kind of funny that you call her Aunt Gayle, but Martin is only Marty and he's the one you're related to by blood."

"I am a firm believer in being able to pick your family. Some of them don't deserve the title."

"I won't argue there. I've had many days where I wished I could pick a different Mom."

"You kind of did."

"What do you mean?"

"Well, you married me and got my mom in the mix. Technically, you got to pick." Flynn winked at me as I rolled my eyes at him.

"Be glad your mom is a good one." I sighed. "I feel bad for Gayle. She has to suffer for her son's and husband's mistakes. It doesn't seem fair."

"No, it doesn't. It would be nice if all the assholes flocked to one another, but they're usually good at picking up on all the shady shit, since they do it too. They have to go after the nice people who aren't looking too closely at what they're doing."

"I never thought of it like that."

"It's not something you have to worry about with me. I bought something at the store earlier," he mentioned and I could tell it was just to change the subject, but I played along.

"I hope it wasn't pie. Your mom's cobbler was delicious, but I think I had way too much."

He had the audacity to laugh at me. "No, it's not pie. It's belly butter."

"Belly butter?"

"Yeah, you know, like a special kind of lotion for pregnant bellies. I thought, since we found out we're having twins, we should probably do what we can to take care of your skin. It's going to stretch so much with our babies."

"Are you saying you won't love me when I'm all stretch-marked and loose-skinned?"

"I'll love you no matter what your outer package looks like, Courtney. It's not your body I'm in love with."

I gasped and stared at him as he watched a tear track down my face. "You said you're in love with me."

"I am."

"Are you sure?"

He grinned at me before he turned back to the task at

hand. Thankfully, we were almost home. Once I got him in my arms, it was debatable whether I'd ever let him go again.

"I am positive. No matter what, I will love you just the same - more when I watch as you bring our children into this world because that is a miracle I can't perform."

"Are you trying to make me cry?" I blubbered from the passenger seat.

I could tell my husband was trying not to laugh at messy hormones, but he wasn't doing a great job at hiding it. "Not unless they're happy tears."

"Of course they are. Why would anyone be sad to have you love them?" I grabbed a fast-food napkin out of the glove box and blew my nose into it. "I love you too, you know."

"I know you do."

"No, I mean, I've been falling in love with you too."

"I know," he told me assuredly, as if it was old news and not something I'd never said to him before.

"How in the hell would you know that?" I asked and then promptly blew my nose again. We had come a long way from me not wanting to walk across a room naked in front of him to my utter lack of care about what he saw. I also blamed that on the pregnancy.

"You told me."

"I told you?" I let the question hang in the air for a minute, even though I saw him nod his head in answer. "When in the hell did I do that?"

"Remember that night you got really drunk and I had to pick you up from that biker bar?"

"Yeah," I dragged the word out slowly as I attempted to piece together where he was going with that.

"You had a lot to say on the ride home before you passed out."

"Oh!" I hid my face by looking out the window but my a flush of heat burned from my cheeks to the tip of my ears with embarrassment. "Did I say how long I'd been in love with you?"

"No." His answer sounded a bit more like a question, in that I could tell he wanted to hear more. When I didn't add on, he decided to come out and ask, "Do you want to elaborate?"

"Not really," I huffed. I was surprised when he didn't push for the answer, but then again, my husband wasn't one to force things. He didn't mind waiting for them to come in their own time, and I loved that about him.

FLYNN RUBBED the sweet honeysuckle scent into my belly as I laid back on a stack of pillows on our bed. "Are you going to do this every night?"

"Yes," he answered.

I moaned and aimed a sweet smile his way. "You're the best husband I've ever had."

"I'm the only husband you've ever had."

"You set the bar pretty high for yourself, though." He shook his head at me, but I could see that he loved my answer. "You still owe me a date night. That disastrous family dinner doesn't count."

"Okay, where would you like to go? We'll have date night tomorrow."

"You don't have to work late?"

"Sweetheart, I won't be working late nights again for the foreseeable future."

"Why not?"

"You're pregnant. I want to be here for you as much as possible. When you're no longer pregnant, we'll have two infants at home who require so much attention that they'll need both of us on the job. When they grow to be a bit bigger, we'll have two toddlers throwing tantrums about snacks, toys, and whatever toddler show they're into. You're going to need a break from the chaos, so I want to be there. We're also going to have date nights, because we need to be there *with* each other, and not just for one another."

"How did I get so damn lucky?" I asked Flynn. He shrugged his shoulders as he finished buttering up my belly. "All done?"

"For now," he whispered.

"Then why don't you come up here, so I can make out with my hot husband?"

"Oh yeah?"

"Wait!" I called out as he started to crawl up the bed toward me.

"What?"

"You should totally do that naked."

My husband humored me and stood there on the bed to undress instead of getting down on the floor like a normal human. I laughed as he took off each piece of clothing and did a silly little dance and hip thrust before slinging each piece around in circles and letting them land wherever.

"You're cleaning the mess up," I warned.

"Worth it to see you smile like that."

I sat up and ripped my bra off, but when I reached down

to pull my little shorts and panties off, Flynn stopped me. "I want to unwrap my beautiful wife."

I couldn't argue with that, so I watched as he gripped the sides of my shorts and slowly slid them down my hips. He kissed my legs the whole way down as he pulled the shorts away. Then he moved back up to repeat the process with my panties, only he started with a sweet open-mouthed kiss to my mound before he ever moved the silky material down.

"You're a tease," I joked as he slid further down and kissed my thighs, then my knees. I felt him chuckle against my skin and it sent goosebumps across my body.

"You like it," he taunted as he touched the places where the bumps erupted. Once my panties were off, my husband worked his way back up my legs then pushed them apart so he could get closer to my center. His tongue swiped right up my middle and then teased my clit with the barest of strokes across it before he blew gently to cool me right back down after the heated licks. The sensation shift made me shiver.

Flynn grinned up at me and then repeated the process. I never would have thought him barely touching my clit could send me shooting off like a rocket, but it did.

"That was something," Flynn suggested as his smile grew wider.

"It's the hormones," I teased.

"Nothing to do with my skill, huh?" he asked.

I laughed but shook my head no at the same time. "Okay then, we'll have to see if I can change your mind." He moved me so that the front of his body spooned my back and then he put a pillow underneath my leg in such a way that it stayed propped up higher while his leg pinned my other one down. Then, he thrust his cock deep inside me and I cried out for every deity I could name to make it so I never had to stop feeling this good.

"Mmm, you don't need to call the gods, sweetheart. Just tell me what you want."

"More. You. Always. Don't stop." Each word was panted out as he thrust hard into me.

"You like this?" Flynn questioned. "Want more of my cock inside you?" He tweaked my nipple as he asked, and I cried out once more.

"Yes, Flynn. Give me more."

"Okay, sweetheart." He picked up his speed and thrust into me over and over at a relentless pace. My pussy clenched around his cock and dripped in a way it never did when I wasn't pregnant. We made a mess of the bed, and then after we caught our breath, he had me ride him until I couldn't go anymore. Then he fucked me from behind until we both came and I promptly passed out.

There was no denying the fact that I loved my husband, but even if I didn't, I don't think I could give up sex with him for anything.

I HAD BEEN LOOKING FORWARD to our make up date night all day, but my bladder had other ideas. For the second time since we sat down to eat, I had to get up and go pee. When I approached our table, there was a woman standing there talking to my husband. He had stood up at some point, and I can only imagine it was to give her a hug.

"I have to say, I didn't expect to see you out tonight, but

I'm glad we ran into each other," the woman said as I drew closer.

"Yeah? Why is that?"

She seemed puzzled by his reaction for a minute and then shook off whatever doubt my husband just caused. "Well," her finger traced up his chest to his shoulder, and I swear she was trying to get to his jaw to trace that too, but Flynn took a step back away from her. Again, she furrowed her brow in question but continued right on.

"Well, it's been more than a year since we've seen one another and quite frankly I miss you in the bedroom."

"We never met in a bedroom," Flynn corrected.

"Right you are. Always were the naughty one and up for a bit of anything."

"Is there a point to this?" Flynn asked her in a bored tone.

"I thought I made the point. I want to hook up, but this time, maybe we can turn it into something more."

"No."

"No?" she questioned, clearly taken aback by his abrupt dismissal.

"I said no. I'm taken."

"Well, you don't have to be taken," she hinted.

That was when I stopped dallying. I didn't think my husband would take her up on her offer in a million years, but the bitch was boring me and causing a scene, especially since the people who had been dining near us knew he was there with me.

I worked my way to Flynn's side and slid my arm around his waist and then pressed my hand that wore the wedding band up to his chest, so that it was right in her face.

"Hi, do I know you?" I asked the woman.

"No," she huffed.

"Oh, well then, I'm sure you need to get back to your own table." Flynn smirked and then nodded his head. "Julia, this is my wife, Courtney." He held me close and placed his hand on my belly, which made it very obvious that I was with child."

"You knocked someone up?" Julia was a bit loud with that shocked revelation.

"Yes, my *wife*!"

"Wait, you were already married? As in, she didn't baby trap you?"

"Julia, you need to leave now. As you so crudely pointed out, my wife is pregnant and very hormonal. Speaking to you, even in a friendly manner, considering what you just proposed is not going to happen because I won't risk upsetting the mother of my children. To answer your question in more blunt terms, I do not want to hook up with you again now or anytime in the future. My cousin, Beckett, is free though if you're looking for a subpar replacement."

I giggled aloud because my husband didn't even realize how true that statement was.

"I thought you two were only friends. Aren't you the girl who dated Beckett for like ever?"

"I was that girl, but now I'm his wife. No hard feelings. If I was in your shoes, I would have taken the shot too."

Julia left after that, and I sat back down at the table with Flynn. "I'm a little disappointed," my husband said to me as he laughed.

"How so? Would you rather hook up with her than have to go home to me and my ever-expanding waistline?"

He chuckled and shook his head. "No way. I'm disappointed that you weren't ready to throw down and fight for your husband's honor."

"Did you forget that I am currently making two humans? I barely have the energy to walk back to our table from the bathroom, let alone take on one of your past hookups. Besides, you did a damn fine job all on your own. Remind me to reward you for that later." I winked at him, then I remembered he stood up to hug the bitch. "You lost points for hugging her though."

"I didn't stand up to greet her originally. She leaned down to get a hug, and it put her tits level with my face, so I jumped up to avoid that scene."

"Oh, good save, baby."

"About those rewards…"

"What about them?"

"What kind are we talking about here?"

"The kind that involves you watching me sleep if you don't hurry up and order our desert."

"Yes ma'am!" he laughed as he signaled for our waiter to come back to the table.

Chapter Twenty-Five

FLYNN

"I NEED you to say that one more time, only slower." I stared down at the phone and waited to hear my sister tell me about how our father arranged a marriage for our youngest sister.

"You heard me right the first time," Bea groused.

"Dad knew I couldn't get that money until I'd been married for at least six months."

"My best guess is that he couldn't wait. Maybe marrying her off was always his plan. I don't know."

"What does Mina have to say about it?"

"She agreed to do it. I don't know why, but Flynn, something has been going on with her for a while now and I'm worried. I think she's using this marriage as a way to hide from everyone."

"I'll find the time to go talk to her."

"How do you think Courtney will feel when she finds out that Mina saved Dad's business, and your marriage wasn't necessary."

"Fuck, Bea. My marriage to Courtney was for nothing then."

"That's an awful thing to say."

"I wasn't done, asshole. I meant that she had to give up her life for me. Her whole relationship crashed hard all because Beckett convinced her to help me save my dad's business."

"Yeah well, if you ask me, she got the better end of the deal anyway."

"No doubt. I'm a definite upgrade to Beckett."

I heard a crash and Courtney screamed. "Gotta go." I called out as I ran from my office. "Courtney?"

"Flynn, what's going on?" Bea called through the phone. Dammit, I needed her to hang up in case I had to call 9-1-1. "Hang up, Bea!" I ordered as I found Courtney lying on her side, curled up in a ball at the top of the steps.

"Courtney!" I yelled. I dialed the fucking number I dreaded having to use and tried to check my wife over, but she curled deeper into a ball when I did.

"Court, I need you to tell me where it hurts, so I can tell the dispatcher."

"Go away, Flynn."

"No can do."

It only took a few minutes for the ambulance to arrive, and I had to go downstairs to let them in. Once they got Court loaded up, I was told I had to take my own car because there was no room, but I didn't think that was why. The way the ambulance crew looked at me, it was clear that they wanted to get my wife alone to see if I had abused her. I understood even as I resented the implication.

It didn't look good, especially since Courtney kept flinching away from me for some reason.

When I got to the hospital, the woman at the front desk informed me that I wasn't welcome to join my wife. "What do you mean, I'm not welcome? I'm her fucking husband!" I shouted.

"And she requested that you not be allowed back."

"She's pregnant with twins. I need to know that they're all okay. Her and the babies."

"I'll check to see if she will allow us to share that information, but you're still not allowed to go back."

Bea made it in time to hear what the woman had to say to me, and she pulled me aside. "Oh God, Flynn, what if she overheard our conversation?"

"So? I would have told her anyway."

"No, what if she only heard part of it?"

"I don't get why that would be upsetting."

"Imagine you're pregnant with twins and deeply in love with your husband and their father." I smiled at the thought. Up until about an hour ago, that was exactly what I thought. "Now imagine you overhear your husband telling someone on the phone that your marriage to her was for nothing."

"Fuck, are you serious?"

Bea shrugged. "Unless you did something else that was incredibly stupid, it makes sense."

"Can you go back and talk to her?"

"I can try," my sister agreed.

IT TOOK three hours before Bea made her way back out to the waiting room. I put in the call to Courtney's dad, but he was out of the country and said he would catch the first flight back. I didn't bother to call Jill because I thought she might make matters worse not better.

"Hey," Bea called out to me. I jumped up to meet her, but she shook her head and hustled my way instead. "They're keeping her overnight for observation to make sure she and the twins are okay. She ran from the exact conversation I told you was the problem."

"Okay, but you explained the situation, right?"

"I did, but she got hurt as a result of what she overheard. I don't think it quite sunk in that it wasn't what she thought. Either that or she thinks I'm lying for you." Bea shrugged her shoulders. "The good news is, she doesn't have a concussion and the doctor thinks she only has a bit of superficial bruising and a spot or two of deep tissue bruising. It's near her hip and radiating out toward her belly, which is why they want to monitor her. The doctor assured us that it looks worse than it is."

"Jesus fucking Christ, Bea. I can't lose her. I can't lose any of them. How the hell am I supposed to convince her that she's the love of my life when she's lying there, alone, thinking I regret marrying her?"

"I'm going to head back in, but you might as well go home to wait because she hasn't changed her mind."

"I'm not leaving until she does."

"Okay, I'll let her know."

"Bea, tell her how much I love her. Please, make her believe it." As my sister walked away, I had to swipe the tears away that blurred my vision. How was it possible that my wife was hurt, in the hospital, and I couldn't even see her, check on her, or be there for her?

Bea never came back out and eventually I fell asleep, curled up in a ball, on a series of three very uncomfortable plastic chairs. If I was smart, I would have gone out to the car to sleep, but I didn't want to take the chance that my sister would come out to the waiting room to get me if my wife changed her mind about seeing me.

Someone tapped on my shoulder. I felt it again before I managed to come fully awake. I groaned as my body shifted on the hard chairs in an attempt to get up. "Fuck, that hurts," I grunted.

"Flynn?"

Her voice woke me the rest of the way up immediately. "Court? My Nemesis?" I asked as I took her in. She stood in front of me looking beautiful as ever, even if her face was puffy from crying about overhearing the wrong fucking thing and probably the pain from her fall as well.

"Bea was going to take me home, but since you're here, you can save her the trip."

"I told you it wasn't a bother," my sister admonished.

"Go home, Bea." She rolled her eyes at me and mumbled something about gratitude. "Thank you for staying with her," I called out. My sister waved her hand and continued out the door as Courtney stood there staring at me. "Right, sorry." I jumped up and immediately landed back down on my ass in the chair as my dead leg gave out on me. The minute I thought about it being asleep, the pins and needles sensation started.

"Ow! Ow! Ow! Fuck the blood flow." I heard a giggle

and looked up to see my wife laughing at me. "You think it's funny?"

"It's not - not funny," she insisted.

"Give me a minute to get the blood flow back and I'll help you out of here."

She was seated in a wheelchair that my sister had been pushing. "Did you guys steal the wheels?"

"No. It's hospital policy to be wheeled out, but we were already in the hallway on the way to the elevator when some alarms started to go off in one of the rooms. The nurse told me to wait, but Bea took off with me as soon as my nurse ran into that room."

"Nice, my sister broke you out of the hospital." It felt good to be able to joke around with my wife after a night of wondering if we were over. "Court, you know you didn't hear everything-"

She cut me off with a shake of her head. "Let's wait for that conversation until we're home."

Once we got to the car, I helped Courtney in and then pushed the wheelchair up on the sidewalk. We were nearly home before my wife spoke again.

"Bea told me that you've been in love with me since we first met."

"That's true."

"Why didn't you ever say anything?"

"Because you were with Beckett, and I thought you were happy."

"There were times when we broke up," she reminded me. "That one time…"

"I would have taken you from him then, but he showed up and you followed him off into the sunset again. I loved you. I fucking loved you enough to go along with whatever made you happy, even if it was my fucknut cousin."

"I wish you wouldn't have."

"No use looking back, Court. We can't change any of it."

"I know. There are just moments when I wonder what it would have been like to not waste all that time on a man who never deserved it."

"Can we talk about the real elephant in the car now?" I asked and she gave me a lopsided, goofy grin.

"Are you talking about me," she pointed down to her burgeoning belly, "or the fact that I overreacted after eaves-dropping?"

"You are a gorgeous Goddess, Nemesis. No elephant could ever compare. I was talking about the fact that those words ever came out of my mouth. I know you thought I meant it like I was saying it for myself, but I just meant that you would have probably made a different choice if it wasn't for my family's circumstances. Honestly, you might have never even known I needed to marry to gain access to my inheritance."

"That's true, and I already know all that, Flynn. I'm sorry. I heard what you said and my heart broke. I shouldn't have run. I should have stayed and faced it, because then I would have heard the rest of what you said. The consequences were that I almost harmed our babies. If I had slid a little bit further..."

"No use dwelling on things that never happened, sweetheart. We can't change what went down, and we won't dwell on what never was. Okay?"

"Okay. I'm not sure it's going to be so easy to turn those thoughts off, but I'll try."

"I love you, Courtney. So fucking much. Don't ever doubt that."

"I know. I'm sorry. I won't"

"We talk things out. Running doesn't work, obviously, because you can't stay upright on your feet." She laughed at my dumb joke and then her eyes went really wide, and her cheeks and ears turned pink.

"Damn you, Flynn!"

"What did I do?"

"You made me pee my pants a little."

I couldn't help it. I laughed and then my wife hit me in the gut, but she laughed too, and the sound made everything okay again.

Chapter Twenty-Six

FLYNN

I sat in the chair beside my wife's bed and held our youngest son. Ryker William Robeson was born second, and he came screaming into the world where his brother had been stoic and needed to be coaxed into showing off his lungs for us.

Courtney went into labor five weeks early, but the twins still weighed around five pounds each. I glanced up to see that she was done feeding our oldest boy, Rylan Jacob Robeson.

"Switch?" I asked. She grinned and nodded to me. I gently laid Ryker across her lap and then took Rylan from her.

"Don't forget to burp him," she reminded me.

"Whatever you say, Momma."

I grabbed one of the burp cloths and threw it over my shoulder. It was a lesson I learned after the first feeding when my son threw up inside my shirt. "Is he still being a pain in the butt about latching on?" I asked.

"A little, but I think he's finally getting the hang of it."

"We get to go home tomorrow. Are you ready?" I continued to pat my son's back as Courtney's eyes swung up to meet mine.

"We'll have privacy again, which will be nice. I'm a little scared of not having professional backup in case something goes wrong, though."

"We'll be okay, and if not, Mom and Aunt Gayle are on tenterhooks waiting to swoop in and save the day so they can have grandbaby time."

"I'm grateful that Gayle wants to be in our lives considering everything my mom did."

"Your mom didn't have an affair by herself. Marty was a willing participant."

"I know, but she has to hate me, at least a little. If it wasn't for my relationship with her son-"

I cut her off there. "Nope. Your parents and his were friends for a long time, before you two even knew what dating was. I love you, sweetheart, but you have to stop taking responsibility for everyone else's bullshit."

"You're right, and you need to figure out new words before our boys start to talk. There's no way I'm dropping them off at their Grammy's house one day to tell her all about the bullshit they got into at home."

I quietly laughed with my wife until someone wrapped their knuckles gently on the door. I moved to open it and found my parents standing there. "We weren't sure if it was okay to come up or not."

"Of course, it is. Come on in."

"We found a straggler in the hall on our way up," my mother said. I glanced behind my dad to find Reed there.

"Hey Reed, come on in. There's plenty of room."

"Oh, this is perfect," Courtney said as she started to burp Ryker. I was glad she had finished up because I didn't even think twice about the fact that she was breastfeeding. "Dads," my wife called out. That got both of their attention. "We would like to introduce you to your grandsons."

"What am I? Chopped liver?" my mom asked. I chuckled and held my finger up to my lips to tell her to be quiet for a minute.

Courtney grinned at my mom, gave her a wink, and then turned her attention back to our fathers. "We want you to meet, Ryker William Robeson," she called out and her father's eyes immediately misted up.

I moved in closer to my own dad. "And this little guy is Rylan Jacob Robeson."

"Are you serious? You named him after me?" my dad asked.

"Both of our boys got their middle names from their grandfathers. The men who helped to mold us into the people we are today." My dad swiped at his eyes about the same time Reed did. "Do you want to hold your grandson?"

"Are you kidding? I thought you'd never ask!" my mother swooped in and stole my oldest son right out from under my dad.

"Snooze you lose?" I questioned.

"I know better than to stand between your mother and a brand-new baby."

"Smart man," I told him.

"Happy wife, happy life," he threw back at me. I didn't miss the way Reed's face fell at the declaration. The fact that his wife cheated wasn't on him. That was a choice she made, but he obviously felt it deeply.

"Love you, Dad," I heard my wife tell him.

"Love you too, baby girl. Real damn proud of you. These are some fine boys you brought into the world." Reed turned to me then. "Maybe next time, you try for a little girl. I swear to you, she will be the joy of your whole damn life."

Courtney sniffled and then started bawling so hard her dad had to take the baby from her. I went to the bathroom and grabbed some tissues for her. "You okay?" I asked as the grandparents pretended they couldn't hear us while they all three fawned over the boys.

"Happy tears," she whispered as she blew her nose and let the tears fall unchecked.

OUR FIRST NIGHT HOME, we stood over the boys' crib staring at them as though we were to look away they would poof out of existence. At least, that's the reason Courtney gave me. I couldn't believe we made two perfect little humans together.

"We're going to need to buy a much bigger house."

"Why?"

"Because I already want to get you pregnant again."

She laughed like I was joking. I wasn't. Her dad's comment earlier lit a fire in my brain that had already been on a slow simmer. When Courtney saw that I wasn't laughing with her, she turned serious.

"I just gave birth to two of your children at once! I think we can wait a while."

I smirked at her. "We'll see."

"Flynn, you're going to see when you're neck deep in shitty diapers and squalling babies."

"I can't wait," I told her as I leaned in and kissed the top of her head. She wrapped her arms around my waist and snuggled close.

"I love you so much, I'm almost crazy enough to agree with you."

"As soon as the doctor green lights your health, Nemesis."

"You're going to need a new nickname for me soon."

"Why is that?"

She shrugged. "I haven't felt particularly vengeful lately, considering I have everything I ever dreamed of."

I squeezed her into a tighter hug. "I think we'll hold off on a name change until the first time someone insults one of our boys. I have a feeling Momma Bear is going to be one tough-"

"Cookie," she cut in to say. It hadn't been the word I would have used, but hers sounded better.

"Exactly what I was about to say."

"Sure, pal. Come on, we need to sleep when they do," my wife whispered. We both tiptoed out of the room and just as we pulled the door shut halfway, one of my boys decided, "Fuck naps!"

"Well, we tried," Courtney huffed. We had to laugh. It was still funny on day one of being alone with them.

There was no need to talk about how the next eighteen years with twin boys went for us, though. The bright spot was that they became their little sister's protectors and I didn't have to worry so much about the dumb boys trying to run games on my little girl.

THANKS FOR READING A Different Husband, book #3 in the Robeson Family Novels

Please read/review the book, as this is how other readers find the books you love.

Don't forget to check out the other books in the Robeson Family Novels.

- The Forgotten Wife
- When the Last Petal Falls

Thank you for reading

For new release news, updates, book recommendations, bonus content, and ARC opportunities, sign up for my newsletter:
https://christineandanne.myflodesk.com/newsletter

If you enjoyed this series, you should read:

Bad at Love

Christine Michelle

About the Book:

POSIE

I fell in love with the idea of Maxwell Carter when I was too young to understand just how that beautiful boy would break my heart one day.
I was never his best friend.

Never a girlfriend.

We were strangers turned pen pals.

Through those letters, we each grew more complicated feelings, especially since he never actually came home to see me in person.

Maxwell was bad at love, and I had to let the hope of ever being with him go.

I managed that right up until a very special person in both of our lives brought us back together in an unexpected way.

MAX

Pops used to give me what he called "woman advice."

When I was younger, I blew it all off, thinking I knew everything there was to know about the opposite sex.

Failed relationship after failed relationship proved I should have listened to the old coot before it was too late.

It wasn't until I came back to my hometown at thirty-three that I realized the most important thing he tried to convey to me. The love of a good woman – the perfect woman for me – had been in my grasp all that time, only I'd failed to see her for what she was until it was too late.

I was finally coming home, and she was free once more.

Both of us were a little worse for the wear, but Pops' lessons had finally sunk in, and I wouldn't stop trying until I finally made her mine.

Chapter 1

Posie - 16

His lips were so close, I could almost taste them. My heart was stuck somewhere in my throat as his tongue darted out and slid across that plump lower lip that captivated me in the strangest ways.

"Kiss me." It was a demand that made my heart clench tightly in my chest, almost like it would stop and never start again.

My eyes shuttered themselves, so I wouldn't have to see. For some horrible, sick reason they wouldn't stay shut. When my eyes opened again, it was to see his hand in her shiny blond hair as their mouths came together in a sensual dance I'd been dreaming of experiencing for years. Only, those weren't my lips he was tasting. It wasn't my hair that he gripped so tightly in his fist that I could imagine exactly what it would feel like.

It was, however, my heart that cracked wide open at having to witness their kiss so closely. Knowing you're invisible to the one person who holds your heart in their hands is bad enough, but he didn't even realize I was there in the same space with them. I'd come up here to escape another one of my mother's dark rages. Everyone thought she was so sweet. The town baker, who made fabulous cookies and cakes and sold them with a smile on her face every day, couldn't possibly be a monster at home.

She didn't use to be, not until my father died. Now, my only solace was to come to Jack Carter's farm and hide away in his barn. It was slightly embarrassing that he knew about my crush on his grandson. Nothing near as painful as watching Max kissing Cheyenne. She'd never been outright mean to me or anything, but I was just as invisible to her as I was to Max. That was saying something, considering she and I shared three classes, and we were on the volleyball team together.

I rubbed my hand over the center of my chest, where everything felt far too tight as they continued kissing. Each smacking sound that came from them, every moan and heart-wrenching sigh made it feel even tighter until the barn door opened. Jack stuck his head inside and called out my name.

"Posie, you in here?"

Max and Cheyenne quickly pulled apart, their attention going to Jack, whose eyes travelled from them to my own.

"What's going on, Pops?"

"What in the hell are you doing in my barn, boy?"

Max seemed stunned by his grandfather's angry response to seeing him there. "Don't answer. I can see for myself what you thought you were doin'. This ain't a hotel for you to bring your latest girlfriend to."

Cheyenne gasped at the implication that she hadn't been the only one. Truthfully, I didn't know if that was the case, as this was the first time I'd run into Max here.

"You two need to go," Pops insisted before his eyes ghosted back to mine briefly, the worry there tore at my heart. Unfortunately, that one look made Max turn my way. His eyes grew wide when he finally noticed me there in the corner with my sketchbook and my headphones on. His eyes quickly shifted down to Cheyenne, who was still clueless to my presence.

"Shit," Max huffed before he grabbed his girlfriend's hand. I was so jealous of that touch. If I closed my eyes and imagined it was me in her place, I could almost feel the heat of his touch against my palm. When the tear fell down my cheek, I couldn't even move to brush it away without drawing more attention to myself. Instead, I allowed it to fall unhindered without looking up to see who may have noticed.

"Pops, I didn't know," I heard Max say.

"Just go, boy." After a few minutes, I heard the engine of Max's old Chevy rev. It was odd that I hadn't heard him when he arrived, but then again, I'd had my music cranked up pretty loudly when I first came to hide out in the barn. Jack sat beside me as I thought about it, and he patted my knee.

"Bad day, Posie?"

The nod of my head was the only answer I could offer because my throat felt like it was too tight to form a response. Jack sighed and then reached over to swipe away the tears that ran down my cheeks, but it did no good. The tears refused to dry up.

"Sorry," I muttered.

"What in the hell are you apologizing for?"

I shook my head back and forth, not knowing how to answer that. "I didn't hear them come in. I came to get away and," my eyes dropped to the sketchpad in my lap, "try to forget."

"What did she do, Posie?"

I shook my head again. "I'm sorry that I didn't say anything to them when I realized they were here, but they didn't see me, and by the time I noticed them, it would have been embarrassing." We sat there quietly for a moment before Jack pulled me into his side and let me cry. "No one ever really sees me, so I just stayed invisible, Jack." The admission was so quiet, I didn't know if he really heard me or not.

"Posie," he started to say when the door of the barn slammed shut and I wasn't sure who had been there. "Sweet girl, seeing you like this breaks an old man's heart." Jack held me like that for a while before he stood and held his hand out to help me up.

"Come on, let's go get you cleaned up and I'll make you some supper before you have to go home."

Chapter 2
Max - 17

One minute, I was making out with my girlfriend in my Pops' barn. The next, he was yelling at us to get out. Pops never yelled at anyone, least of all me, so it was a shock to my system. Then he made it sound like this might be a regular occurrence for me, and Cheyenne stiffened in my arms, her accusing eyes lifted to meet mine as they pleaded silently for me to tell her it wasn't true.

I was about to be disrespectful to my Pops for the first time in my life when I caught his eyes looking past where we were sitting in the hay that had been piled up. My eyes followed his line of sight, and I was shocked as hell to see there was a girl sitting there with her knees pulled up damn near to her chest. The only thing stopping those two parts of her body from meeting was a notebook.

She looked somewhat familiar, though I couldn't place who she was or why she might be in my grandfather's barn. It didn't matter that she was a stranger. My heart lodged in my throat as I watched a single tear track down her face.

The girl looked so fucking sad that I could feel it in my own soul. Her dark eyes shuttered closed for a moment as her head tilted down to shelter herself from being seen.

"You two need to go," Pops said, drawing my attention back to him.

"Shit." The word slipped free before I could pull it back. I got Cheyenne out of there before she even noticed that there was another person in the barn. There was no way to tell how she would have reacted to another girl being there, especially after what my Pops had said in anger. I jumped in my truck and started it up before I realized Cheyenne stood there staring at me like I'd grown two heads.

She huffed and then moved to the car that was parked on the other side of my truck. Fuck! That was going to go over like a ball of fucking lead. I forgot she met me here because she had to meet her parents in town later.

"Cheyenne," I called out to her as I hopped back out of my truck.

She flipped me off and left. That was going to require some groveling to fix later. Right then, curiosity got the better of me instead of worries about my girlfriend. I moved quietly back into the barn to observe whatever the fuck was going on with the stowaway in there. Pops had called the girl by name, so she wasn't just some random kid crashing in his barn.

I stuck to the shadows and creeped close enough to over-hear what they were saying.

"What in the hell are you apologizing for?"

The girl removed her headphones as she shook her head, causing the light brownish-blonde locks to fall further into her face and obscure my view of her. "I didn't hear them come in. I came to get away and," her eyes dropped to the sketchpad in her lap, "try to forget."

"What did she do, Posie?"

What the hell could that mean? Cheyenne hadn't even known she was there. I was about to step in and tell Pops that before this little waif of a girl made up stories to go with her fake tears, but her head slowly did that back-and-forth motion again, almost as if she didn't even realize she was answering him that way.

"I'm sorry that I didn't say anything to them when I realized they were here, but they didn't see me, and by the time I noticed them, it would have been embarrassing."

I watched as my grandfather pulled her into a hug, as if she was one of his own kin. It was weird to see, since I still didn't even know who the hell she was.

"No one ever really sees me, so I just stayed invisible, Jack."

Damn. I might not have known the girl, but once again, my heart ached for her. What the hell had she been through to make her feel that way? And who in the hell was she to my grandfather? I couldn't interrupt them to ask Pops, so I turned and left, knowing someone who might be able to tell me something. Unfortunately, I wasn't as stealthy on my way out because I tripped and the barn door ended up slamming shut, giving away the fact that I'd been there.

The whole way back to my house, I couldn't get the look of the girl's tear-stained face out of my mind. The sadness seemed to weigh her down and make her appear smaller than she probably was. Then again, being all bunched up and hidden in the corner like that didn't help much.

"Dad!" I yelled the minute I got out of the truck. I'd

seen him under the hood of my mom's car. There probably wasn't anything wrong with it. He just liked to tinker on engines. Still, his head popped up immediately and his grimy face offered up a bright smile in contrast as he flashed me his pearly whites.

"What's going on Max?"

"We need to talk about Pops," I stated.

The smile slipped from his face as he closed the hood of my mom's car and started wiping his hands on the rag he had hanging from his back jeans pocket. "What about Pops?" he asked. Then, as if an epiphany hit, he chuckled. "Let me guess? He caught you taking your girl to the barn?"

"How in the hell?" Was the old man psychic or what?

Dad kept right on chuckling. "Son, your fly is down, hair's a mess, and if I'm not mistaken, that's hay you have on your shirt."

"I guess nothing gets by you," I tossed back, full of sarcasm. "Except maybe that Pops is keeping a sad little mouse of a girl in his barn."

"What did you just say?" my dad asked, obviously stunned by what I'd thrown at him.

"She didn't even make a peep to let Cheyenne and me know she was there. Just watched us making out and…"

"And?"

"And she was crying." For some reason that admission made me feel equal parts guilty and responsible for those tears, even though it was in no way my fault that she was squatting in my Pops' barn.

"You didn't by chance catch the girl's name, did you?" my father asked, and for the first time, I realized he wasn't all that surprised.

187

"Pops called her Posie."

Dad nodded his head and started walking toward the porch. "Let's go sit down while I explain a few things to you."

I followed along, suddenly worried about having left Pops there alone with the girl. I wasn't worried he was being inappropriate, but maybe that she might be taking advantage of him.

"Do you remember Eric Gamble?"

"The guy that was killed in the combine accident on the farm across from Pops'?"

"That's the one." Dad stared at me, as if that should be answer enough to all the questions I had. When I didn't clue in, he sighed heavily. "He left behind a wife and daughter. Max…" Another heavy sigh blanketed the pause before he looked me directly in the eyes. "What I'm about to say is not fodder for school rumors, you hear?"

"Yeah."

He waited a moment, assessing me, as if he didn't believe that I'd keep whatever he had to tell me quiet. The sincerity in my eyes must have finally swayed him because he leaned forward with his elbows on his knees, after taking a seat in one of the chairs. He promptly set his chin on his fists and then sighed again.

"Eric and I were good friends. We grew up across the street from one another and often helped out on one another's farms when it was required. We were best friends for a long time."

I didn't know that. "What happened?" I asked because Alex Cole was my dad's best friend since my earliest memories.

A small smile split his otherwise serious face for a minute. "Your mom happened."

"Mom?" A light started to dawn on the topic. Former best friends and my mom. "I'm guessing you won the battle for her heart?"

"There was never really a battle. We saw her at the same time, but she immediately gravitated toward me. I was, uh, sort of seeing someone at the time. So, Eric thought he had a shot with Sharon."

"You cheated on someone to get with Mom?" I asked, unable to believe it because my parents always preached to us about loyalty and staying true to the one you loved. I'd never been in love, so that hadn't ever been a lesson I did more than role my eyes at.

"No. I broke it off with Sue before I ever took your mom out. Honestly, Sue was a lot to handle, and we were already hell and far gone from a healthy relationship, if you could even call it that. We dated, she would throw wild, jealous fits if anyone else talked to me, even if it was innocent. Anyway, I broke it off with her and started seeing your mom. Eric didn't take it too well because he'd had a thing for Sue before she and I got together.

"Long story short, because it was the second girl I'd started dating that Eric was interested in, he thought I was doing it on purpose."

"That's dumb."

Dad shrugged his shoulders. "He had some pretty big voices in his ear back then, telling him that was the truth. One of those voices turned out to be Sue's. Son, you need to understand, what I thought was over-the-top jealousy from her was a lot more. Sue and Eric ended up getting married after he got her pregnant. It wasn't long after their son was born that he came to me and apologized for the accusations and the damage he'd caused to our friendship.

"It was a little too late at that point. I'd written him off, especially since he was with Sue. We remained cordial and friendly after that, but never really worked at putting a true friendship back together because Sue was dead set against it." Dad took a breather, and I sat there wondering what in the world all this history had to do with Pops and the girl in his barn.

"When their boy was two, he drowned in the bathtub while Eric was out working the fields. Sue claimed that she just left the baby for a minute to go get a towel, and that she slipped and hit her head, knocked herself out. Eric came home and found her on the floor and the baby in the tub. When they realized what happened, Sue supposedly lost it and was institutionalized."

"Supposedly?" I asked.

Dad nodded his head slowly. "Most people think she killed their baby and pretended to be injured, especially since she refused medical treatment and there weren't any visible injuries to suggest her story was true. No lump, no blood." He shrugged his shoulders. "I told you she struggled a lot, even more so after they had that baby. It wasn't a farfetched idea that she might have hurt him."

"That's wild."

"When she came back to town years later, around the time your mom was pregnant with you, I thought Eric would finally give her the divorce papers he'd had drawn up. I think he did at some point. Hell, he was dating another woman by then."

"He dated someone else while she was in the hospital?"

"It wasn't like that. No one begrudged him that. Eric was at the top of the list of people who thought Sue killed his son. He had to wait until she was of sound mind to take her to court for the divorce though. Everyone told him to wait so it could be done properly, but no one wanted him to be stuck in limbo. Sue coming back made things hard on Eric's relationship. She did everything she could to sabotage them. Eventually, she even ended up pregnant again."

"Well, it takes two to get pregnant," I suggested.

"Yeah, it does, Max. It doesn't take two *willing* people though. Sue waited for his girlfriend to leave the morning after a party they'd been too. Eric had been drinking heavily. She, um, went inside and took advantage of the situation. Eric was heartbroken when he realized who was in his arms when he finally woke up. Hell, half the town was heartbroken for him because they all knew what happened. Eric deserved to be happy with his girl."

"Who was she?"

"Doesn't matter. The minute she found out; she dumped him because she couldn't take it anymore. It had been more than a year of putting up with Sue's antics by that point. Then, when Sue announced to the whole damn town that she was pregnant with Eric's child, his girl left town."

"Holy crap, Dad. That's insane. Why didn't anyone do anything?"

Dad's heavy exhale spoke volumes. "We tried. Hell, I think most of the town was in Eric's corner, wanting to prosecute Sue for what she did. It was rape, plain and simple. He kept her there, for the sake of the new baby on the way. When the girl was born, Eric took care of her. If he was in the fields, so was his baby girl. That child never was left alone with her mom. Eric allowed Sue to stay, to be a part of her daughter's life, because her doctor finally got her on some medications that helped with her issues, and he didn't want his daughter growing up without her mom."

"Seems like any kid would be better off without a mom than having one like that."

"You would think, but Sue was a good mom to her. It was obvious she loved her girl. The medication really did help."

"So, what does all this have to do with the girl in the barn."

My dad raised a brow at me, as if to ask if I was really that dumb that I hadn't put it together yet. I figured the girl was the one he was talking about, but that didn't explain much.

"Since Sue had so many issues before, certain contingencies were put into place, just in case anything ever happened to Eric. My father was named her guardian, and ready to step in, should Sue become incapable of caring for her daughter. Dad didn't think he needed to step in when Eric was killed because Sue had been doing so well. I'm guessing, if Posie was crying and hiding away in his barn, that all might be about to change."

"So, what? Pops will take her on as his own kid?" That seemed a little ridiculous to me, but after hearing the whole story, it was honestly all a bit much to swallow anyway.

"Yes, and if Pops isn't able to then I would step up, as I am next in line to take her if anything were to happen."

"You said you and Eric were no longer close."

"I did. When Sue was away, we were able to repair our

relationship quite a bit. We were never as close as when we were kids, but our family was always someone Eric could trust and come to, no matter what. I was there when he put the legalities together and he asked that I step in for Posie if Pops was not here or unable to."

"Why Pops?"

"Eric's father left when he was in middle school. Your pops helped his mom figure out what to do with the farm until Eric could take over. He taught Eric everything he could, and he lives right across the street. The road literally splits their farms, so Pops was able to keep an eye on the place, and on Posie."

"Sounds like you dodged a bullet when Mom came into the picture."

Dad chuckled. "I tell that woman nearly every day that she saved me from crazy. Not that I was planning on sticking around with Sue, but if there was ever a woman who could scare even the craziest woman away, it's your mom."

"I'll take that as a compliment," Mom said as she joined us on the porch. The windows were open, so she'd probably been listening in the whole time. "I'm guessing things aren't going so well for Posie?" she asked my dad.

"I'll check in with Dad later," he assured her.

"If I need to get a room together, I can."

"I think the tough old coot has it covered, but I'll let him know we have a room here, in case he isn't up to it."

My parents were both amazing people, and maybe I didn't get the gene, because I silently hoped the sad girl who hadn't bothered to tell a couple she was there in the barn with them wouldn't be coming to stay with us. From what I'd seen, she might be crazy just like her mom.

Playlist

The Heartbreak Songs

Get Over You - Dylan Conrique
Break My Heart - Matt Hansen
Hold Me Like You Used To - Zoe Wees
Play Dumb - Sam MacPherson
Crying Over You - The Band CAMINO & Chelsea Cutler
Friend - Gracie Abrams
I'll Break My Heart Again - Mimi Webb
Unbearable - Tyler James Bellinger
Kiss Me Goodbye - DeathbyRomy

The Love Songs

I'll Never Not Love You - Michael Buble
One Day Less - Anson Seabra

Also by Christine Michelle

CHRISTINE MICHELLE

Robeson Family Novels

The Forgotten Wife · When the Last Petal Falls ·A Different Husband

Standalone Novels

The Groupie Journal

Letters to Lily

His Bittersweet Regret

Bad at Love

TFO

The Fortunate Ones

T.I.E. Series

The Infinite Something · The Infinite Beat

Valhalla Rising

Revived

Kings of Anarchy: New Mexico

Property of Bigfoot

Aces High MC – Dakotas

Dancing with Danger · Whiskey Tango Foxtrot · The Restart and the Remedy

Aces High MC – Charleston

The Other Princess ·A Love So Hard · The Princess and the Prospect · The Killing Ride ·A Twist of Fate · Everlasting ·A Year and a Day ·The Broken Beginning – Part One ·The Broken Beginning – Part Two

Aces High MC – Tallahassee

Crushed

Aces High MC – Sierra High

Walker · Trouble

Aces High MC – Cedar Falls

Redemption Weather · Proven · Smoke and the Flame · Redemption Duology Box Set

S.H.E. MC

Angel Girl · JoJo · Keys

Dark Leopards MC (paranormal)

Ridden by Darkness · The B Team

Mirage Island Mates

Into the Grasslands · Beyond the Grasslands

Seasons Pack Series

Winter Wolves

The Ancients Series

Shadows of the Ancients · Falling into the White · Branches of the Willow · Bound by the Moon

Vukodlak Brew Series

Entwined · Enraged

The Awakening Series

Birthrights · Revelations · Incarnations

Death Viewers

Breathless

Upper YA Titles

The Voodoo Follies (PNR)

Catch a Falling Star (Dystopian Romance)

About the Author

Christine Michelle (also known as: Anne Storm) runs on coffee and giggles as she writes her angst-fueled romance stories (motorcycle club, rockstar, paranormal, college, & other contemporary as well as women's fiction and marriage in trouble novels).

She is a mom to four humans (2 girls, 2 boys – all grown now).

When she's not writing books, she enjoys reading, drawing, hiking, or feeding her soul with live music at concerts.

Christine is a traveler and has lived all over the USA (and

other parts of the world). She currently lives in San Antonio, Texas with her two fur babies.

Buy direct from me:

https://christineandanne.com/

Sign up for my newsletter:

https://christineandanne.myflodesk.com/newsletter

Universal social links:

https://linktr.ee/christinemichelle

facebook.com/M00nlitDreams

instagram.com/christinemichelle_annestorm

tiktok.com/@christine.michelle.books